BENEATH
THE
DESERT
Sun

NEW YORK TIMES BESTSELLING AUTHOR
KAYLEE RYAN
USA TODAY BESTSELLING AUTHOR
LACEY BLACK

Cover Designer: Book Cover Boutique
Editor: Hot Tree Editing
Proofreader: Kara Hildebrand, Deaton Author Services, Sandra Shipman , Julie Deaton, Joanne Thompson & Jess Hodge

BENEATH
THE
DESERT
Sun

Chapter 1

Chad

THE LETTER IN MY BAG IS BURNING A HOLE THROUGH IT, BUT I promised I wouldn't read it until I arrived at my new base.

I almost caved. When I got on the plane, sitting alone in a tin can full of strangers, all I wanted to do was pull it out of the zipper compartment and read her words, but I refrained. Maybe it's because I knew she'd know. Somehow. Ever since I first met her fourteen months ago, she had an uncanny ability to read me, to see past my cocky smile and find the real me I hid from almost everyone behind witty humor.

Faith.

The one I left behind.

I push all thoughts of her out of my head as the Uber pulls up in front of Fort Cavazos, my new base, as of 0600 tomorrow morning. The moment I step out, the sweltering Texas heat wraps her hands around my neck and slowly applies pressure. This kind of heat is familiar, yet different from growing up in Kentucky. There, it would be hot and humid in the summer. The type of humidity that made it hard to breathe and clothes cling to your body in the worst way. That's not too far off a description of the muggy air in Texas, yet it still feels…off.

Before I can dive into the whys, the MP steps out of the guardhouse.

"Specialist Chad Anthony reporting," I say with a salute before handing over my transfer papers.

The man in the military uniform scans his clipboard before taking my document. "You're to report to Colonel Martinez's office," he states, handing back my papers. "Up this road and to the right. We'll take you."

Another MP steps forward and gets in the Jeep parked along the guardhouse, so I follow suit and climb inside. We don't have time for idle chitchat as we speed away, heading in the direction of the colonel's office. The Jeep stops in front of the large building, and without fanfare, I grab my duffle bag and head inside.

The cool air conditioning hits me the moment I enter. It only takes me a few minutes to go through the security process before I'm escorted down a long hallway to where I'll meet Colonel Martinez.

"Enter." I hear in a low, clipped voice after I knock on the door.

"Specialist Anthony, sir. I was told you wanted to see me, sir," I state once I've saluted the base commander.

"Of course," he replies, leaning back in his chair as he levels me with an intense gaze. "Welcome to Fort Cavazos. Unfortunately, your stay with us will be a rather short one. You're being sent to Fort Irwin in California where you'll join the 11th Armored Cavalry Regiment, Blackhorse. You will be promoted to corporal upon your arrival. You ship out immediately," he states, causing my mind to swirl and my heart to skip a beat.

Corporal.

"Yes, sir," I state, standing at attention.

"See Sergeant Holmes out front for your transfer orders. Dismissed."

I salute the man who was supposed to be my commanding officer but is now sending me on my way to another base. In another state. To do another job.

My mind reels as I receive my new orders and I'm sent to catch a ride to the airport. Even though the letter I carry is still weighing down my bag like a brick, I won't open it until I arrive in California and find out exactly what my new orders are.

But that doesn't stop my brain from thinking about her the entire time.

When I board the plane, I close my eyes and see her long brown hair pulled up high on her head. Her sleepy green eyes sparkling in the morning light as they focused on me. The sound of her laugh, and how it quickly became my most favorite sound in the whole world. The way I miss her, even after all this time.

Faith is my best friend's twin sister.

Never in a million years did I expect to meet a woman who'd challenge me so much when I went to visit his hometown over fourteen months ago. Ford's family lives in Cooper, Ohio, and while we were on a two-week leave, we split our time between his family and mine. That's when he met and fell in love with my cousin, Shayne. I teased him relentlessly, even though I was pretty excited about the whole thing. It happened so quickly. They met, and I watched my best friend fall in love within a matter of days.

Then, we had to leave my hometown in Kentucky and go to his before returning to base. He didn't want to go. No, I take that back. He wanted to see his family, but he didn't want to leave Shayne behind. He did, because that was the job we signed up for, but it was hard. And not just on him, but on me too. I hated watching two people I love hurt the way they did when they were apart, but they made it.

Ford discharged at the end of his four-year commitment and returned to Ohio to be with Shayne. She just completed cosmetology school and is getting ready to take her state license exam, which I know she'll pass with flying colors. Shayne may not have had the best upbringing, but with that pain comes determination, and she was determined to not fall into the same lifestyle her mother had, fueled by drugs and alcohol. With Ford in her corner though, she was bound to succeed.

And she did.

They're going to be moving into a house together near the salon she was hired at. If you would have asked me before that trip almost fifteen months ago, I never would have thought my best friend would fall in love and build a life with my cousin, but they did.

That's also when I met Faith.

My first thought had been…she's gorgeous.

Stunning, really.

The fact she was single was shocking, but the more I got to know her over those next few days, I realized she was single by choice, not because of lack of opportunity. She was getting ready to start her final year of college, and that's where all her focus was directed.

When we met, she was home for the summer, even though she was taking a few online summer classes. I've never hit it off with a woman the way I did Faith, and like Ford and Shayne, our time together was too short.

However, unlike Ford and Shayne, we decided not to pursue a relationship.

What's meant to be will find a way.

That's what she said to me in a tearful goodbye in the early morning before I left to return to base, and what I've hung on to for more than a year since.

We've remained friends, and it's been both heaven and hell. Heaven because I still have her in my life. Someone who makes me smile and doesn't mind when I'm in a bad mood after a long-ass day. In fact, she's usually the one who can turn my mood around. But it's the latter I find myself focusing on the most. Being this far away from her, wanting to touch and hold her again, has been agony. We spent one real night together in that hotel room, but never took it farther than holding each other and stealing a few kisses.

Okay, a lot of kisses.

Leaving her at that hotel was the hardest thing I've ever done to this day, and since then, I've thought of her as the one who got away.

Even if we are still friends.

I'm crammed between a young woman and an older man on my flight from Texas to California. When you're six-one, it's hard to get comfortable in these seats, especially when you can't extend your legs out very far. Fortunately, the flight isn't too long. The woman, probably in her early twenties, spends her time on her phone watching videos, barely looking up to acknowledge the flight staff, while the older gentleman appears to be sleeping. It's at this moment I cave and reach into the pocket of my uniform for the folded piece of paper. I transferred it from my duffle bag to my breast pocket before I boarded, wanting to feel her words close to my chest.

With a sigh, I open the paper and smile at her beautiful penmanship.

Dear Chad,

If you followed directions, you will be in Texas by the time you read this, but I'm guessing you caved somewhere along the way. You're always a bit impatient. ;)

Last night, you told me you were being shipped to Texas, away from Ohio, and that news hit me hard. You might not have realized just how hard, because I smiled and swallowed the tears I nearly cried but somehow managed to keep at bay. Oh, who am I kidding? You probably read me like a book. Like always, right?

Anyway, when I got back to Ford's house, I went to my room, sat on my bed, and let the emotions I felt wash over me. Anger, because you were moving farther away from me, not closer. Fear, because every time I think about you in a combat situation, I'm terrified something will happen to you. Sadness, because I might lose our sporadic phone calls and text messages. Loneliness, because now I'm finished with school and thinking about my future, only to have you taken from me.

But all of those equal me being selfish. Fortunately, there's one emotion stronger than all the others, and that's pride. Like I was when my brother enlisted and left for boot camp, I'm so proud of what you're doing for our country, even if it scares me a little too. Okay, it scares me a lot, because at the end of the day, I want you safe.

Now that I've had time to process the news you shared, I'm just numb. Don't get me wrong, I'm so extremely happy for you, but I'm a little bummed for me. I feel like we were so close, and now we're so far away. Those weekends I had hoped to steal away will be harder to plan. I'm not telling you this to make you feel guilty. I'm telling you this because you're the person I seem to want to tell just about everything to anymore, despite the fact I've spent the last year living with Shayne, who quickly became my best friend. Yet, at the end of the day, I always thought of something to share with you. A story from school. The way some guy cut me off in traffic and I gave him the bird. The new restaurant I discovered late at night when I was studying.

I'm going to miss you. Just like I have every day for the last fourteen months. I know we decided to be friends and "what happens, happens," but just know not a day goes by I don't think of you and wonder where you are or what you're doing. Maybe someday things will be different. I'll always hope for that day.

Be safe. Be happy. I'm so proud of you.

Love,
Faith

I read it a second, then third time, soaking up every word she writes and committing it to memory. It's crazy how you can miss someone with every fiber of your being. Someone who isn't technically yours, but somehow seems to own your heart anyway.

I've never told her to wait for me.

Never.

That's the ultimate selfish dick move.

Don't get me wrong, I've wanted to. So many times, I've wanted to beg her to wait, but that wasn't fair to either of us, even if that particular scenario worked out for Ford and Shayne. I just keep holding on to "what's meant to be will find a way" and praying she doesn't meet someone along the journey. I wouldn't blame her if she did, but I'll always hold out hope.

Her words make me sad. To know we were close, as she said, but now farther away guts me. But this is what I signed up for. This is what I was meant to do, what I had planned to do with my life. Timing has just been a cruel bitch ever since Faith strolled into my life. Or more specifically, since I strolled into hers.

"A letter from home?"

I fold the piece of paper back up and slip it into my pocket. "Yes, sir," I confirm, offering a small smile to the older man sitting beside me.

He nods, knowingly. "A woman, I take it."

I confirm with another small grin. This one's sadder than the first.

"I remember when I left for Vietnam. My Junie was home in Indiana, and it killed me to be apart from her all those months. All I could think about was getting home so I could marry her," he says with a sad look in his eyes. Something instantly tells me his Junie isn't around anymore.

"How'd you do it?" I ask, instantly wanting to reel the question back in. It's not my business or my place to ask such a personal question. I'm ready to tell him to forget I asked, when he replies.

"It wasn't easy, son. We didn't have these telephones in our hands like you kids do nowadays. We had to write letters to communicate, but it was those letters that got me through. I didn't get them nearly as often as I would have hoped because it took forever and a day to move mail all the way over to Vietnam, but when I did," he says, shaking his head gently, a smile turning his lips upward, "it was like I won the lottery. I'd read her words and know I could get through anything. I'd read them at all hours of the day and carried every single one of her letters in my breast pocket of my jacket so they were close to my heart."

I can't help but smile.

"Being apart isn't easy, but the reward is worth the temporary heartache you feel," he adds as we receive the announcement to prepare for descent. "Knowing someone is home, waiting, is one hell of a motivator."

His words hang heavy in my mind. We both follow the flight attendant's instructions, and before I know it, wheels are down in California. It's such a surreal feeling. I started my morning in Texas, ready to get settled at my new base, and I'm suddenly landing in an entirely different state for the same reason.

I release my seat belt when instructed, and the older man beside does the same. Then, he extends his hand. "Sergeant James Conover, US Marine Corp."

"Corporal Chad Anthony, sir," I reply, giving my new title a try.

The old man gives me a firm shake. "Pleased to meet you," he says before releasing my hand and opening the overhead storage compartment. We wait until it's our turn to disembark the plane, and when we're up, he faces me once more. "Thank you for your service, Corporal."

"It was an honor to meet you, sir."

"Same," he says, before turning and walking down the aisle.

I make my way to baggage claim to retrieve my duffle bag, ignoring all the eyes tracking my movements. I've noticed a lot of people take notice of a military person, but they rarely say a word to them. I'm pretty sure I can count on one hand how many times someone has approached me and thanked me for my service. Not that I do this for the accolades or the pomp and circumstance.

I do this for the betterment of my country.

For my future and for those I love.

Just when I throw my bag over my shoulder, I spot a man and woman approach the old man. They have a little girl with them, maybe five or six years old, and as soon as he sees them, he drops the handle of his suitcase and throws his arms around the trio. I can't help but stop and watch the exchange.

When he releases his family, he picks up the little girl, while the gentleman grabs the luggage. They start to walk away, but suddenly the older man stops and faces me. He gives me a big smile, raises his hand, and salutes me. I do the same and wave goodbye, feeling a little lighter than I did before.

I don't know what's in store for me.

I don't know what will happen with Faith.

I don't know where I'll end up next in this big world.

But I do know I'll always carry her with me, wherever I go, whatever I do.

And maybe someday we can be together.

It's that thought, that hope, I hang on to as I step through the sliding doors, into the hot California sun in San Bernardino.

Next stop, Fort Irwin National Training Center.

A bubble of anticipation erupts in my chest at the change in destination and job. I can't wait to see what awaits me with the 11th Armored Cavalry Regiment. It's going to be weird to be here, to do it without my best friend, Ford, but I'm ready.

This is my destiny.

Chapter 2

Faith

I**T'S BEEN FORTY-EIGHT HOURS SINCE HIS FLIGHT LEFT. THAT'S** the last I've heard from him. While I know he's safe, I'm still worried. I can't seem to help myself where Chad is concerned. I might be keeping him at arm's length, but that doesn't mean I don't care about him.

Shaking out of my thoughts, I grab my laptop so that I can continue looking for jobs. I've been accepted as a substitute teacher at our local school here in Cooper and the surrounding areas, but I want to have my own classroom and students.

I'm currently living with my twin brother, Ford, and his fiancée, Shayne. Shayne and I were roommates before my brother left the Army, and she insisted that I live with him instead of moving home with my parents.

I have to admit the thought of moving home didn't sit well with me. Don't get me wrong. I love my parents. They're incredible, but once you have a taste of freedom, it's hard to go back. Not that they would butt into my business, too much, but it's just my childhood bedroom makes me feel as though I'm still a teenager. Besides, I'm only here until I find a teaching position and start getting a regular income. Then, I'll find a place of my own.

Needless to say, I took them up on their offer. I'm hoping that it's only going to be for the rest of the summer, but right now, the job search is looking grim. I'm making it sound worse than it is. I've applied to several schools and even have a few offers, but they're not the offers I was hoping for. I want to teach kindergarten. Yes, I'm aware that I'm being super picky, but that's what my heart is set on. I know that I should just accept and hope that a kindergarten spot becomes available, but as I sit here applying to more schools, branching out a little farther than I originally hoped, I can't help but send up a silent plea that what I'm looking for will fall in my lap.

My phone rings, and I jump at the sound. I grapple to grab the device and end up knocking it off the bed. Tossing my laptop to the side, I slide off the mattress, grab the phone, and swipe at the screen. "Hello," I say in a rush.

"Faith?" Chad's deep voice wraps around me like a warm embrace. "Are you all right?"

"Chad! Hi! Yes, I'm fine." I huff out a deep breath as I try to calm myself down.

"What are you doing?"

"Now? Or when you called?" I ask.

"Both." He chuckles. "Tell me about both."

"Well, when you called, I was searching and applying for jobs."

"And now?" he prompts.

"Now, I'm sitting on my bedroom floor, trying not to be a heavy breather into the phone."

"I'm going to need you to explain that to me, darlin'," he drawls.

Damn, I miss him. "Fine." I sigh dramatically, and I can already practically see him smiling in my mind. "When my phone rang, I had to wrestle the comforter for it, and I lost the battle. The phone slid off the bed, and in my attempt to get to it before it stopped ringing, I ended up on the floor too."

"Are you okay?" I can hear the concern in his voice, and my heart clenches in my chest. I miss him so much.

"I'm fine. Better now that I'm talking to you. How's Texas?"

"It was fine."

"Was? I'm going to need you to explain that to me, darlin'." I pitch my voice to attempt to sound like him. I fail miserably. Chad's voice is deep and sexy, and yeah, I don't even come close to replicating it, but he gets the point if his laughter is any indication.

"As soon as I got there, I was told I was being transferred and given a new position."

I swallow the lump in my throat that has suddenly appeared. *Please don't let him be overseas. Please don't let him be overseas.* I chant the words over and over in my head. "Where are you?"

"California."

"Oh." I heave a sigh of relief. "That's great, Chad. Congratulations! How's California?" I ask, trying to mask the fear that was just coursing through my veins.

"It's too far away from you. From Ford and Shayne," he quickly adds.

"But you're on US soil. It could be worse." I pause, taking another deep breath, attempting to gather my composure. "You have to give me your new address. I have letters and care packages to send."

"Already?" he asks.

"Are you really surprised?" I ask.

"No. Not the least little bit." He chuckles. "Thank you for the letter."

"Did you wait?"

"Kind of. I made it all the way to Texas, but on the plane to California, I caved."

My heart races knowing he read my letter. I opened my heart to him. "I knew you would." I'm smiling. "Although, I am impressed that you managed to make it to Texas and on the next plane before you caved."

His deep laugh wraps around my soul. "Tell me about your job hunt?"

"Well, I've been approved as a substitute from a laundry list of schools in Cooper and the surrounding area."

"And a full-time position?" he prompts.

"I've been offered a few," I confess.

"Faith! That's incredible. Do you know which you want to accept?"

I pause and decide to give him the truth. I've never lied to him, and I won't start now. "None of them. I mean, I don't think any of them. They're just not what I want, Chad."

"What do you want?"

You. I swallow my gut reaction. "I want to teach kindergarten. It's been my dream, and I know that I'm being irrational. I know that with teaching, you don't always get the exact grade that you want, but I really want kindergarten."

"Then you hold out for what you really want."

"Yeah, I know, but then I'm living with Ford and Shayne rent-free, I might add. They're just starting their life together, both of them out of school and out of the service, and I'm here like the third wheel that I am. I need to find a job and find my own place."

"Faith, you know that they don't give two shits that you're living with them. In fact, I know Shayne is happy that you're there. She loves being roommates with you."

"Yeah, but now she's marrying my brother, and I'm sure they want their alone time together. I just...I'm feeling so overwhelmed.

My heart wants one thing, but I know in my mind that taking any position with a good school to get my foot in the door is the way to go, but I just can't seem to accept any of them."

"How long until you have to give them an answer?"

"The end of the month, so three or so weeks. Give or take a day or two."

"Take a few days to think about it. Talk to Ford and Shayne. Talk to your mom. I'm sure she has great advice."

"I have. She told me that sometimes I need to get my foot in the door and hold out until the class that I really want opens up."

"I know you have your heart set on kindergarten, and I have no doubt that's where you will end up."

"Yeah," I say softly.

"Listen, I need to go. I have to get settled and grab some food. I have to report at 0400."

"Okay. Stay safe and send me your new address."

"I will. Call or text anytime. I'll reply when I can."

"I know the drill."

"Just making sure you know that I might not be there, but you're here with me. Always."

Hot tears prick my eyes. "I miss you."

"I miss you too. Get some rest."

"Night."

"Night, sweetheart."

The line goes dead as the tears fall. Glancing at the clock, I see it's midnight here, so it's nine in California, I think. Hopefully, he can find something to eat this late and get in bed. I hate to think that my whining about my job search kept him up too late, where he'll be tired tomorrow.

Over the job search for tonight, I stand from the floor and grab my laptop, placing it on my nightstand. I'll start my search over again tomorrow. Sliding beneath the covers, I close my eyes and will sleep to claim me. Only, it never comes. Over an hour later and I'm still staring up at the dark ceiling. Reaching over, I turn on the lamp, grab the notebook and pen from the nightstand, and begin to write.

Chad,

> *It's late. Well, after one in the morning. I can't sleep, and since you have to be up at the ass-crack of dawn, and I can't call you, a letter it is. I'm really struggling with this job situation. I have three offers. One from Cooper Elementary and two from surrounding elementary schools. All three are good schools, in good neighborhoods, and not a far drive from Cooper.*
>
> *I hate that I'm being so difficult, but my heart is telling me to hold out. It feels as though I'm settling, even though I know that's not the case. I'll still be a teacher, still helping to shape young minds, just not the new young minds I was hoping for.*
>
> *Anyway, I hope that you're settling in well. I miss you. Be safe.*

Love,
Faith

Closing the notebook, I place it on the nightstand as a reminder to drop the letter in the mail tomorrow. Turning off the lamp, I snuggle back beneath the covers, and finally, sleep claims me.

I'm back in my room, hiding from my brother and best friend. I'm once again scouring the internet for jobs when my cell alerts me to a message.

> **Chad: Can you talk?**

> **Me: To you? Always.**

I've barely hit Send when my phone rings. "Hey," I greet him.

"It's good to hear your voice."

"It hasn't even been twenty-four hours since we last talked."

"Too long."

"How was your day?"

"Long, exhausting, overwhelming. This new position is more re-sponsibility, and while I'm thrilled to be given the opportunity, there's a lot to learn."

"You're going to be amazing, Chad. You're hard-working and ded-icated, and I have no doubt you're going to be kicking ass and barking orders in no time."

He huffs out a laugh. "How about you? How was your day? Any luck with the job search?"

"Nope. I've applied for a few more. I've also been researching the three schools that offered me positions. Creeping on their websites and social media. Just trying to get a feel for each of them."

"That's a good idea."

"I don't know why I'm letting this stress me out so much. I should be thrilled that I have three offers to choose from. It's not that I'm un-happy, but I really had my heart set on kindergarten."

"I think you should take a step back. Take a break for a few days. Don't look at jobs or research schools. Just chill and try to clear your mind. Maybe then you'll feel more confident in your decision."

"Yeah, maybe you're right."

"Of course I'm right."

"That does sound nice, but it's not like I have a job and am rolling in the dough to take a trip."

"Come to me."

I freeze. Pulling the phone away from my face, I make sure we're still connected. "What?" I ask, placing the phone back to my ear.

"You heard me. Come to California. Visit me. I'll rent you a room and buy you a plane ticket. Come here and enjoy the sunshine of the West Coast for a while. Clear your mind."

"I can't just come to California."

"What's stopping you, Faith? It's the summer, you're not committed to a job yet, and it's California. I have the weekends off for now, except team workouts, and we can spend a day at the beach."

"Are you even near the beach?"

"Yeah, well, kind of. Closer than you are," he teases. "I heard some of the guys talking tonight, and Moreno Beach is just about one hundred miles from where I'm stationed."

"That's a long drive."

"But it will be with me."

"We'll get there and have to turn around."

"No, we can leave early, then spend the night, and drive home early the next day."

"That's a lot of driving when we could be visiting."

"Babe, we'll be together the entire time. Come on. It will be fun."

"We don't have to go to the beach."

"Fine, we can do whatever you want. We can lock ourselves in your hotel room for all I care. We can have dinner each night and then explore the area on the weekends. I haven't had time to do that yet. I need you here to experience it with me." His voice is pleading, and I admit seeing him already has a strong appeal.

"I can't let you buy me a ticket and a room. I have money saved up."

"I can and I will. Look, I've saved almost every dime I've made while enlisted. I can afford to bring you out here, and I want to see you. Please say yes. I'll take care of it all right now. You'll have the details in your inbox within the hour."

"I don't know." My heart gallops inside my chest. Can I really just pack up and go see him for a few days? I miss him like crazy, and honestly, I'm not doing much here right now. Excitement bubbles up inside me.

"Come on. Come to California, clear your head. Even if you get a position, I know you, and you won't be taking any time off except for school holidays that teachers don't have to come in for. You're too dedicated. Please."

"You really want me to come and see you?"

"Yes." No hesitation.

"I do miss you. I miss your hugs."

"Then come to California and get one. I promise to smother you in hugs while you're here to tide you over."

"You drive a hard bargain." I bite down on my bottom lip while I process what he's asking. I would love to go see him. I've never been to California, so that would be a new experience as well, but the biggest appeal is Chad and his hugs.

"Only for things I really want."

"You promise lots of hugs?"

"Unlimited," he says, hearing the excitement building in his voice.

"I can buy my ticket and room."

"No. I asked you to come to me, and I'm paying. Let me do this, Faith."

"Okay." My voice is soft.

"Really?"

"Really. If you're sure."

"Fuck yes, I'm sure. When? When can you be here?"

"I've got nothing holding me back. You tell me when to be there, and that's what I'll do."

"How long? How long can you stay?"

"How long do you want me to stay?"

"All summer?" he asks, hopefully.

"That's going to be an expensive hotel stay."

"Damn," he mutters. "I wish you could stay on base with me."

"It's fine."

"I need at least a week. Seven days."

"Okay."

"Wait, two weeks. Yeah, two weeks."

I laugh. "Why don't you check on the prices of hotel stays and flights and then we can decide. Even if it's one night, it will be worth it to get to see you."

"Oh, hell no. It's going to be longer than one night."

"Okay. Just let me know when you get it all figured out."

"You're really doing it? You're coming to California? You're coming to me?"

"I am."

"Fuck. I miss the hell out of you."

"I miss you too."

"Okay, I'm hanging up now. I'm going to find a room and a flight. I'll have it all worked out within the hour."

"It doesn't have to be tonight." I smile, even though he can't see me. It makes my heart happy that he's so excited for me to come and visit.

"Yes, it does. I'm not giving you the chance to change your mind. The ticket will be nonrefundable. You have to come to see me."

I can picture the big grin on his face.

"I won't change my mind."

"Good. I'm going to go. I'll call you back in a few."

"Okay."

"Stay by your phone."

"I'll keep it on me," I assure him.

"Fuck yes," he says as the line goes dead. I can't help the giggle that escapes just as there's a knock at my bedroom door.

"Come in," I call out.

Shayne sticks her head in the door. "Hey, we're going to watch a movie. You want to join us?"

"Uh, no, thanks, though. I'm waiting on a call from Chad. He's advised me that I better answer."

"I thought I heard you talking."

"You did."

"And?"

"And he asked me to come to California to see him."

Her eyes light up. "And you said yes, right?"

"I did. I've been telling him how stressed I am about this whole job search situation, and he thinks getting away for a few days and clearing my head will help."

"Does he now?" She grins.

"We're just friends."

"Does your heart know that?" my best friend counters.

"I think so." I look down at my phone that's gripped tightly in my hands.

"When do you leave?" she asks.

I'm grateful she let it go. "I'm not sure. He's arranging it all. He's supposed to call me back."

"We can pause the movie when he calls," she offers.

"You don't have to do that. I'm going to wait for his call and go to bed. I didn't sleep well last night."

"All right, well, if you change your mind, you know where we'll be. Oh, and let me know when you need a ride to the airport." She winks and closes my bedroom door.

I think about her question about if my heart knows, and it does. It's all we are and can be right now, but that doesn't mean I don't wish for more. It was a mutual decision for us to see where the future takes us and if it would bring us together as more than friends who kiss, hug, and talk to each other multiple times a day.

My heart knows we're friends.

My heart also knows that we love Chad Anthony.

Chapter 3

Chad

LANDED.

The screen on the wall just changed, which means she's here.

I head toward the baggage claim area, where I told her I'd meet her when she arrived. It's been a long week, despite the fact I've been learning my new job with my new team. Each day has crawled along until it was finally Friday.

When I called her back the other night with details on flights and the hotel, she didn't hesitate. The flight was booked, and the room reserved, both on my credit card, despite her insisting she would cover it.

It was my invitation. I was paying.

Turns out, a small hotel not far from where I work offers a package rate for families of servicemen and women, which was at a decent discount. It's an inn used frequently by visitors and offers the basic necessities for their guests, including a continental breakfast. I was able to secure her a king-size room, and I'll be honest, I'm hoping I'll be able to join her a few times in that bed. But if not, that's okay too. I'm not going to push it. Just having her here for two weeks is enough.

For now.

I can't wait.

I adjust the flowers in my hands nervously. I've never been more anxious in my entire life than I am to see Faith right now, and that's saying something. When I got on that bus to head to boot camp, I was a ball of nerves. A mixture of fear and excitement. Now, it's mostly anticipation, along with a root-deep desperation to see the one woman who consumes my every dream and most of my waking thoughts too.

My eyes keep scanning the crowd, especially when I see a large group making their way toward the luggage conveyor I'm standing near. I spot movement weaving in and out of the masses, politely excusing herself as she buzzes around them to get to the front of the pack. A huge smile spreads across my face moments before our eyes meet, and suddenly, she's running, her slender legs eating up the space between us. I take two steps forward and hold out my arms, ready for what's coming.

Faith leaps, dropping her carry-on bag in the process and slamming into my chest. I catch her easily, forgetting all about the bouquet in my hand, as my arms wrap around her body. I pull her close and just breathe her in. Her legs lock around my back, and I have to ignore the way my cock notices her nearness and focus just on her. On the smell of her shampoo and the way she molds perfectly against me.

As if we were made for each other.

"I can't believe you're here," I mutter, inhaling her sweet scent.

Jasmine.

My favorite ever since the day we met.

"Me either," she whispers, her warm breath tickling my neck.

Finally, she pulls back and gives me that familiar grin. The one that makes my heart pound in my chest and my dick get all sorts of excited. My lips move forward, pressing against her forehead hard. It takes everything I have not to kiss her lips.

I haven't actually kissed her sweet mouth in over a year. Ever since that night we spent in a hotel and decided to press the pause button. That one amazing night where we made out like high schoolers. When I kissed her so much, my lips were raw and swollen for hours after I left her.

Since then, the few times we've actually seen each other, we've kept it PG. Friends don't make out, even though I desperately long to do just that. Friends don't also sport huge hard-ons and picture her sweet face when I'm alone in the shower, either, but we're not talking about that right now.

"Welcome to California," I say, slowly letting her slide off me, knowing she's going to feel exactly how excited I am to see her when she reaches my groin.

"Thank you," she replies, trying to contain her grin as she looks me up and down, taking in my jeans and Army T-shirt. She has yet to step back, to put any real distance between us, which I'm extremely grateful for. If it were up to me, she'd be in my arms and plastered against me the entire time she's here.

I bend down and grab the flowers I dropped, along with her carry-on duffle bag. "What do you have in here?" I tease, feeling the weight of whatever's in the bag.

"A small child," she quips, reaching for the bag.

"I got it," I tell her, extending my hand and holding out the bouquet. "These are for you."

Faith smiles widely as she takes the flowers, bringing them to her nose and inhaling. "I love them. Thank you."

Tossing my arm around her shoulder, we turn and head for the conveyor belt. Suitcases are already dropping as passengers shuffle and retrieve their baggage. I set her carry-on beside her feet and say, "Point out yours, and I'll grab it."

She looks up. "I can get it."

Because I can't help it, I lean down and press my lips to her forehead once more. "You're my guest, Faith. I'll get your luggage."

She merely nods and returns her gaze back to the train of bags slowly moving around the belt. After a few minutes, she points. "That one. The black one with the green ribbon on the handle."

I release my hold on her and step forward, ready to snatch the suitcase as it approaches. Within seconds, I'm wheeling her luggage away from the crowd and picking up the duffle at her feet. "Ready?"

"Yes," she replies, bringing the flowers to her nose once more.

We walk together side by side through the exit and head for the parking garage. I don't know why this feels so right, having her beside me, but it does. Anytime she's near, my world just seems better, more at peace.

I slip a key fob out of my pocket and press the unlock button once we approach. "You have a car already?" she asks as the trunk pops open on the black Chevy Malibu.

"No, I rented it. I wanted you to have wheels in case you want to go somewhere while I'm busy, and since I'm still new to the area and don't know much about the public transportation or ride services, I didn't feel comfortable relying on those," I state, slipping her duffle bag into the trunk and reaching for the suitcase. "Also, we have a decent drive to get back to the base."

"You rented me a car too?" She seems dumbfounded at the fact I wanted to make sure she has wheels while she's visiting.

I bend down to move the large case but stop when she asks her question. Standing upright again, I step forward and meet her gaze. "Yes. You don't have to use it unless you want to. Plus, I thought it would come in handy this weekend."

The corner of her mouth curls upward. "What's this weekend?"

Bending down, I lift the suitcase and slip it inside the trunk. "Not telling. It's a surprise," I state, closing the lid and flashing her a big grin.

Faith rolls her eyes but can't stop the smile. "Fine. Be that way," she sasses, walking around me to get into the passenger seat.

I run around her and open the door. "Your chariot, my lady."

Shaking her head, she slips inside and sets her flowers on her lap. "Thank you, kind sir."

With a quick push, I shut the door and practically sprint around to the opposite side. I give the ignition a start, fasten my seat belt, and throw the car in Reverse. "Your vacation starts now, Faith. Sit back and enjoy."

The drive from the airport to Fort Irwin isn't exactly convenient at around two hours, but it is what it is. That'll give us plenty of time to catch up and talk as we make our way toward the base.

"How was your flight?" I ask, merging with traffic.

"It was good. I sat next to a mother and young son on their way to visit her grandparents. I was worried about him during the takeoff and descent, but he was a rock star. She kept him occupied with a movie on her phone. He didn't so much as make a sound unless he wanted a snack."

"That's great. The last time I flew to Florida, I sat next to a couple whose baby cried the whole time. I felt absolutely terrible for them. They were so embarrassed and getting frustrated, probably because they could hear the complaints from the other passengers. When we were stable in the air, I asked them if they minded if I held him to give them a break. I could see the hesitation along with the relief in both their eyes as the dad handed him over. The baby was so damn tiny. I just cradled him in my arms, stood up, and slowly moved up and down the aisle. Within a couple of minutes, he was out like a light."

When she doesn't say anything, I glance her way for a moment. Her eyes are wide and full of something I don't want to dissect for fear it'll give me too much hope in our situation. "That's the sweetest," she mutters with a soft smile.

I shrug, keeping my eyes on the road instead of on her. "It was the least I could do. They were seriously stressing out. I've heard babies respond to that."

"I've heard the same."

"How's the job search coming?" I ask once we get onto the highway. She sighs and leans her head back against the headrest. "I should just accept one of the offered positions. There are so many good schools looking to fill teaching positions. I broadened my search and found a few kindergarten spots, but they're all farther than I want to drive, which means I'd have to relocate. I'm not against that, but I don't know the area or school system, so I'm just… I don't know, hesitant, maybe?"

"That's understandable," I reply. "It's always a little scary to move somewhere new. You don't know anyone, and the comments online are always mixed."

"Is that how you felt moving here?"

"Yeah. Fortunately, most of the soldiers I've encountered are welcoming and good dudes."

"Most of them?" There's no missing the question within her question.

"There are these two guys who don't particularly care for me. One of them was up for a promotion and I ended up with it. Hell, I didn't even apply for the spot. I was recommended and given new orders when I got to Texas."

"Sounds like something catty women do," she adds.

"Probably. Anyway, unfortunately, I have to deal with them daily, since they're on my team."

"That sucks. Can't you get them moved?"

"Yeah, but I won't. Not unless they are a danger to themselves or someone else on the team. I can deal with their brand of bullshit, which usually is just mumbling stuff under their breath. The other guys just roll their eyes at 'em."

"Well, you're a better man than most," she says.

We chat for the next hour and a half, until I finally see the lights of Fort Irwin in the distance. As I enter the small town, Faith seems to sit up straighter in her seat as she takes it all in.

"We'll go on an official tour this weekend when you can actually see it in the daylight. It's a pretty cool place," I tell her, heading to the center of town where the hotel sits.

I park in the lot and shut off the ignition. "Ready?"

She nods, eagerness filling those alluring green eyes. "Ready."

I step out of the car, Faith meeting me at the back before I can open her door. While I grab her large suitcase, she pulls her carry-on out and slips it over her shoulder. "I can get that."

She shrugs and doesn't make a move to hand over the duffle bag. "I've got it."

I take her hand and we walk through the front entrance. When she realizes I'm bypassing the front desk and heading straight for the elevator, she gives me a curious look. "Don't we need to register?"

I press the Call button, and the elevator immediately opens. "I did that before I went to pick you up," I confess, waiting for her to enter the small car before following her inside.

"You did?"

I nod, refusing to tell her why. She'll see in a few minutes. "You're on the third floor. I wanted to make sure it wasn't on the ground level, because it's statistically the most unsafe floor in a hotel. Not that I anticipate trouble here. I mean, you're near an Army base. Chances are this is one of the safest areas in the state."

The door opens, and she steps out. "What room?"

"Three fifteen," I reply, pulling a key card from my pocket and handing it over. The second one is tucked securely in my wallet.

We proceed down the short hall until we find her room. Faith slips the key card in the door and pushes it open. The room is already lit with soft lighting, since I turned on the floor lamp over by the table when I was here earlier. Aware we'd arrive well after dark, I didn't want her to have to stumble around for a light. I also spot my surprise sitting on the bed, waiting.

I hang back, letting Faith take the lead as she checks out the room. It only takes a second before she notices the extra touches I added to the place she'll be staying for the next two weeks.

She drops her bag onto the floor and walks toward the bed. "What's this?" she asks almost absently to herself as she picks up the note. Once she reads the words, she turns and rewards me with a breathtaking smile. "Thank you, Chad."

"You're welcome," I reply, even though saying more is on the tip of my tongue.

Faith pulls the gifts out of the basket. Sour Patch Kids, Goldfish crackers, and soft caramel candies—her favorites—along with a murder mystery book she's been talking about reading before it comes to the big screen later this year. "I can't believe you remembered," she says, setting the book beside the snacks.

I don't tell her I remember everything. *Everything*.

Next, she grabs the folded piece of paper and opens it. Once she scans the words, she turns wide eyes my way. "This is too much," she insists.

"Never," I state, shoving my hands in my pockets to keep from reaching for her. "I wish this place was a little fancier so you could do that stuff here, but since it's not available, I found it somewhere else. One of the men on my team's wife works there. Her name is Hannah, and she'll do the nails portion of your appointment. He assured me the other ladies you'll see are great at their jobs and very trustworthy."

She turns and heads my way, placing her hands on my forearms. I can feel the warmth in her touch as she goes up on her tiptoes and places her lips against mine in the softest kiss. Every ounce of blood I possess rushes south of my belt, landing firmly in my groin, and despite wanting to take her in my arms and control the kiss, I remain rooted in place.

"Thank you, Chad," she whispers, her breath warming my chin as she gazes up at me. "No one has ever done anything like this for me before."

"You're welcome." It takes all the strength I have not to kiss her again.

She slowly drops her hands from my arms and turns back to survey the room. As much as I want to stay with her tonight, I can't, and she needs time to get settled.

"Do you need anything before I go?" I ask, shoving my hands back into my pockets like a buffer to keep from touching her.

Faith spins around, a look on her pretty face I can't quite decipher. "You're leaving?"

"I had planned on it," I say, unable to keep myself away from her any longer. Taking a step forward, I place one hand on her hip, while the other pushes strands of hair off her forehead. "I have an early morning team workout I have to be at, so I thought I'd let you get settled tonight and maybe sleep in. But I'll be here by noon or so to start our weekend together."

She smiles and relaxes. "Okay. That sounds good."

Again, I step back and walk toward the door. If I don't do it now, I'll never leave. "There's a continental breakfast downstairs, and here are the car keys," I state, removing them from my pocket and setting them on the desk. "I kept the spare key card, but only for emergencies. If you'd prefer to have both, I'll leave it."

She's already shaking her head. "No, you keep it."

With a single nod, I reach for the door handle and give it a turn. "I'll be here by noon," I reiterate, most likely just to add a few more seconds of time with her. "Make sure you use the safety latch when I leave."

She grins as she walks my way. "Yes, *Dad*."

With a low growl, I mutter, "The things running through my head aren't very fatherly, Faith."

"No?" she asks, running her hands up my chest and resting the palms against my pecs.

I shake my head, unable to form words. I'm strung tight with desire, a need for her I'm not sure will ever be sated. "Good night, Faith," I whisper softly.

"Good night, Chad. Thank you again. For everything. I'm really excited to spend these next two weeks with you," she replies, going up on her tiptoes and kissing my cheek.

I'd much rather have her lips on mine like earlier, but I'll take this too.

At least for now.

"Lock up," I insist once more before finally turning the handle and stepping into the hall.

"Night, Chad," she repeats, grabbing the door. "See you tomorrow."

I nod, standing still until she closes the door and I hear the locks engage. Only then do I head for the elevator, preparing for the short walk back to base.

It's late.

Damn late.

Tomorrow morning is going to be brutal, but the lack of sleep will be worth it. Knowing she's here, in California, is worth any loss of sleep I may experience over the next two weeks. I'm going to take advantage of our time together as much as I can, because I know it's limited. Two weeks won't be nearly enough time with her, this I already know, which is why I'm going to make the most of it.

And not think about that final day until it comes.

Because that day will be the one I lose my heart completely.

The day she returns home and takes it with her.

Chapter 4

Faith

As soon as I engage the lock, I make my way back to the king-sized bed and plop myself face-first on the mattress. I don't know what I thought tonight would be, but I didn't anticipate being alone this soon. At least we had the drive, which was two wonderful hours of Chad time. I'm exhausted from the flight and need a shower. However, I know that if I don't touch base with my parents, even though I'm an adult, my brother and best friend will be blowing up my phone and calling Fort Irwin demanding my whereabouts.

Okay, that's a little far-fetched, but I don't want them to worry, and I know they will.

With a heavy sigh, I climb off the bed and go in search of my phone. I decide to call my parents instead of texting. I know if it was me, I'd want to hear their voice. Just like I wanted to hear Chad's.

"Faith!" Mom answers.

"Hey, Mom." I chuckle.

"How was your flight?"

"Good. No issues. Chad met me at the airport, and I just got checked into my room. It's about a two-hour ride from the airport to the base."

"That's what your dad was telling me. He looked it up when you told him where you were staying."

Most girls my age would roll their eyes at that, but me, I just smile. I love that my parents care. When I told them that I was flying to California to visit Chad for two weeks, they told me to be safe, to have fun, to tell Chad hello, and to check in often. It's not a hardship to let the people you love, and that love you, know that you're okay.

"I knew he would." I smile.

"How's Chad?"

"He's good. He's in a new position, which is why he was moved to California from Texas, so he has a lot to learn, but he seems to be enjoying it. He's already back at base. He has something in the morning, but we're going to go out and explore the area tomorrow afternoon. He hasn't had much of a chance to do that since he got here."

"That's good that he doesn't have to do it on his own. I'm sure he appreciates a friendly face to help him navigate his new area."

"I'm sure he would have been just fine without me. He's already made a couple of friends on base."

"Regardless, I'm sure he's glad to see you."

"Yeah," I agree. "It's nice to get to see him too. I hate that he's so far away. Weekend road trips just aren't possible with him in California."

"Your dad says hello," she tells me, but she didn't have to. I can hear him in the background telling her to tell me hi and that he loves me. "And that he loves you," she adds, and I can hear the smile in her voice.

"Tell him I said hello and that I love him too," I say, covering a yawn.

"All right, I can tell you're exhausted from a long day of traveling. Check in with us, please."

"Will do, Mom. Love you."

"Love you too." She ends the call, and I immediately tap on the screen to call Shayne. It rings once on my end before she picks up.

"I miss you."

I can't help it. I laugh at my best friend and future sister-in-law. "I miss you too."

"How is he?"

"He's good. He's getting used to his new position and a new area, but we're going to go exploring this weekend."

"Let me say hi."

"He's actually not here. It was a long drive from the airport, and he has to be up early tomorrow," I explain to her as I did my mom. "He'll be done by noon."

"Damn," Shayne mutters.

"Yeah, but I'm exhausted from the flight and the drive. Poor Chad, he's going to be drained tomorrow."

"He will be, but we both know he wouldn't have changed a thing."

"We're just friends," I remind her.

"Why is that again?" she asks.

"Honestly, I can't even remember. I know we said we would be friends and leave the rest up to life or fate or whatever," I ramble.

"And look at where life led you. You're in California with your 'just' friend."

"I'm visiting."

"And so soon," she jokes.

"I don't know what we're doing. I miss him like crazy, and he's always the first person I want to call or talk to when I have a good day or even a bad one."

"Gee, thanks." She pretends to be upset, but we both know better. My brother, Ford, is that person for her.

"Talk to him, Faith."

"Something is holding us back." I just wish I knew exactly what that something was so I could squash it like a damn bug.

"Something? Or two stubborn humans?"

I sigh into the phone. "I think he just didn't want to hurt my feelings."

"I call bullshit. That man is into you."

"We're friends, Shayne. I know he cares about me, but not the way that Ford cares about you." My heart clenches in my chest as I say the words aloud, but that doesn't make them any less true. I know that Chad cares about me. Hell, I'd go as far as saying that he loves me. He's just not *in* love with me. Not the way I'm in love with him. There's a big difference between the two, and I've decided I'm okay with any part of himself he's willing to give me.

"Stubborn," Shayne mutters, and it pulls a grin from my lips.

"I love you."

"I love you too. Ford's already asleep, the old man that he is," she teases. "I'll be sure to tell him you called. Keep in touch while you're there. Be safe, and maybe pull up those big girl panties of yours and tell Chad how you really feel about him."

"Maybe," I reply, not committing. We both know my "maybe" is a big fat hell no. It's not worth the risk of losing him and making things awkward between us.

"Get some rest. Make sure your door is locked."

My grin widens. "Chad already made sure of that before he left."

"Good man that one," she responds. "Call me and have fun."

"I will. Bye."

"Bye."

Tossing my phone on the bed, I go for the suitcase and dig for my toiletry bag and clothes. I'll unpack tomorrow. Right now, I just need a shower and sleep.

I tossed and turned all night. It's always like that for me the first night in a new place. It doesn't help that I'm here alone. Well, Chad's close, but I was here in this place all on my own. It's not that I was freaked out, but just the idea of being by myself in a strange place kept me awake.

Finally, at a little after seven, I was tired of the game of twister I was playing with the sheets, so I crawled out of bed. I unpacked and organized all of my things, including the basket from Chad, before taking another shower and getting ready for the day.

I ventured out and found a small café and grabbed a large, iced coffee and a bagel with cream cheese before coming back to the room. I wanted to explore more, but I didn't want to miss Chad. He said around noon, but if he happened to be out early and headed this way, I didn't want to miss him.

That brings me to my current situation. I'm propped up on the bed, iced coffee and bagel long since consumed, while I hold my e-reader in one hand, my phone clutched in the other—just in case Chad calls or sends a message.

I'm a romance novel junkie. I devour them and never leave home without my handy little reading device that puts the words of my favorite authors in the palm of my hands. I'm so engrossed in the story—the hero is about to confess his love for the heroine—when there's a knock at the door.

Dropping my e-reader to the bed, I glance at my phone and see no new messages. My heart races with a little fear and a little anticipation. It's just before noon, so a little earlier than when Chad said he would be finished. What if some stranger is knocking on my door? Keeping my steps light as I head to the door, I then stand on my tiptoes and peek through the peephole. Chad's standing with his hands in his pockets, rocking back on his heels.

I pull open the door and smile at him. "Hey. You're early."

"You didn't ask who it was." He frowns.

"I didn't have to. I saw you." I point to the small glass-filled hole in the door. "I could see it was you."

He nods. "Always check, okay?"

"You know I am an adult," I say, crossing my arms over my chest.

His eyes quickly rake over my body before coming back to mine. "I know." His voice is gruff, and I'm suddenly turned on and possibly in need of a change of underwear.

Stepping back, I allow him to enter, before closing the door, and following him farther into the small room. "So, what are we doing today?"

"I have a plan, if you don't have anything already planned."

"Nope. I was waiting for you." I look down at my cutoff jean shorts and tank top. "Am I dressed okay?"

"You're perfect. It's hot as hell outside, and we're going to be outdoors."

"What are we doing?"

"It's a surprise."

"A hint?"

"It's outdoors." He flashes me a wicked grin. The same one that has my belly flutter with butterflies every single time he aims it my way. "I thought we could grab some lunch, and head out. It's about an hour away. Just a little over an hour according to my phone."

"Sure, let me grab my things." Moving back to the bed, I turn off my e-reader, and I know it's a contradiction that I said I take it everywhere, but I'm not taking it today. I don't want anything to take me away from Chad. "You're here early."

"Yeah, we wrapped up early. I might have ridden the guys a little harder than needed to wrap it up." He chuckles.

"They're going to label you as a hard-ass."

He shrugs. "I wanted to see you."

When he says things like that, it makes it harder to remind my heart that he's being a good guy, a good friend. It's difficult to keep the lines between me being head over heels in love with him and our friendship at bay.

I shake out of my moment of swooning over his words, and slide my feet into my flip-flops, grab my purse, and phone then smile at him. "Ready."

Ten minutes later, we're pulling into a small diner in town that screams home cooking, and I'm pumped about it. The bagel I had earlier is long gone. With his hand on the small of my back, the heat from his hand searing my skin through my shirt, Chad leads me into the small diner. We read the sign that tells us to seat ourselves, and he guides the way to a small back-corner booth.

"I love this place already," I tell Chad, reaching for a laminated menu that's kept on the table.

"How do you know?" he asks, reaching for his own menu.

"It smells delicious, and it's literally named Mom and Pop's. You know you're about to experience culinary homemade goodness with a name like that," I tell him.

"I can't argue with that reasoning." He chuckles.

"What can I get ya?" an older lady wearing a black apron, with her hair tied up with ink pens asks.

"Faith." Chad nods to me to go first.

"I'll have the country fried steak, white gravy, mashed potatoes, and green beans, please. Oh, and white milk to drink."

She writes it all down with a nod and turns toward Chad.

"Double that, please," he says, placing his menu back behind the salt and pepper shakers.

"Coming right up," she says, already walking away to put in our order.

"So, you're really not going to tell me where we're going?"

"How am I ever supposed to surprise you?"

"You did. You gave me that basket in my room. That's enough. Please?" I say, batting my eyelashes at him.

"Fine." He playfully rolls his eyes as if he's irritated with me, but the smile tugging at his lips gives him away. He reaches for his phone and taps at the screen before sliding it across the table to me. "We're going to rent a side-by-side UTV and go riding in the desert."

"No!" I say excitedly. "Are we really? Chad! That sounds like so much fun." I wiggle in my seat as I scroll through their website on his phone. Our server drops off our drinks, and I take a quick sip. "Wait, this says you should call ahead for ticket availability."

"I already did."

"Really?" I ask and he nods.

"We have an hour orientation and safety class that we have to take before we can ride, and then they turn us loose in the Mohave Desert."

"I'm so excited. Can I drive?"

"If you want."

"I want." I nod. "This is going to be so much fun."

"I hoped you would think so. It would have been an even better surprise." He gives me a pointed look.

"Hey." I raise my hands in defense. "I can't help it. I had to know."

"I think you would have survived," he tells me as our waitress sets our plates in front of us, grabbing our glasses for refills.

"Then why did you tell me?" I counter.

He scoops up a fork full of mashed potatoes and tilts his head to the side. "Like I could ever say no to you." He shoves the overloaded fork of creamy potato goodness into his mouth while I sit here in the booth with my heart stuttering in my chest.

My mind goes back to my conversation with Shayne last night. Do I have it all wrong? Does he want to be more than friends? No, I'm letting our conversation and his sweet words alter my perception of what I know is real.

"So, a guy I work with, he's a newlywed and I told him my friend was in town. He invited us to dinner at their place while you're here. If you're up for that."

My friend. "Sure, it will be good for you to hang with them and form that bond. I can be a buffer."

"Faith, sweetheart, I'm an Army Corporal in the United States Army. I don't need a buffer."

"Fine, I'll just be the fun friend who also happens to be your best friend's little sister, and your cousin's best friend, from Ohio who missed you so much I had to come and see you for two weeks."

"How about we just tell them you're mine?" My eyes widen, and he's quick to keep talking. "My friend. We don't need to bore them with all the other connections that brought us together."

"That's what you do when you're getting to know someone."

"How about we just leave that for another time?" He chuckles, taking a bite of his country fried steak.

"Fine. I guess I'll just have to tell them all the stories I've heard from Shayne about the two of you growing up."

He points at me. "Behave, woman."

I shove a big bite of mashed potatoes in my mouth so that I don't have to agree.

"So, tell me about the job search."

"Ugh. I'm being dramatic. I know I am. I just can't seem to stop."

"Kindergarten is your dream. Have you considered the jobs that would require you to relocate?"

"I have, but I don't know. None of them feel right. I know that makes me sound like I've lost my damn mind, but it would feel right, wouldn't it? Shouldn't I be nervous and excited? None of the offers I've received so far give me either of those feelings."

"Then you should keep looking."

"I'm a college graduate living with my brother and his fiancée who are soon to be married, if my brother has his way about things. I can't keep cramping their style."

"Did they say you were?"

"No. They would never, but if I were them, I'd want time alone."

"You know good and well as long as the two of them are together, they couldn't care less. They spent too much time apart. They don't give a damn that someone they love is sleeping in their spare room. They're just happy to be together."

"I know you're right. I guess I just thought it would all be different. I'd graduate, find my dream job, get my own place—not paid for by my parents—or a part-time job and a roommate, fall in love, and live happily ever after."

Something flashes in his eyes that I can't name before it's gone. "You can still have all of that. It might not be in Cooper, but you can still have everything you want for your future, Faith."

"No more whining from me. This trip was to see you and forget about all of that for a while."

"Faith, this is a big part of your life right now. Yes, this trip was to get away and to see me—" he flashes me a grin "—but it's also to clear your head to help you make the best decision for you. And that's what you need to do. Choose the path that makes you the happiest. If that's passing on these jobs and subbing until you get your own kindergarten classroom, or if it means you have to move out of Cooper, whatever the end result may be, we all support you as long as you're happy."

And this is why I love you. "Thanks, Chad."

He nods. "Now, finish up. We've got some desert sand to tear up."

Chapter 5

Chad

"I'M NOT SURE I'LL EVER GET ALL THIS SAND OUT OF MY HAIR. HOW was this even possible when I was wearing a helmet?" she asks from the passenger seat of our rental.

I glance her way, a smile instantly spreading across my face. Her hair is matted and rumpled, several long brown strands sticking up every which way. Not to mention the red outline on her face from the goggles. It's cute as hell.

"We had that sand flying everywhere," I confirm, feeling those tiny granules in places you don't ever want them to be. It reminds me of my first tour in Afghanistan with Ford.

"Yeah, but I guess I didn't expect to find it beneath the helmet. And I'm pretty sure I'm taking half the desert back with us in my bra," she states, pulling out the front of her shirt and peeking down at her chest.

My eyes instantly drop to the place hers are focused. "I could help you out with that," I quip, even though I'm totally serious.

She flashes me a wide grin. "I'm sure you would," she sasses, releasing her shirt and kicking back in the seat. She crisscrosses her legs and sighs. "It was totally worth it, though. I had so much fun."

"Me too," I reply, wanting to reach over and grab her hand, entangling our fingers as I drive. But I don't. Sure, I've stolen little touches here and there throughout the day, but nothing as bold as to take her hand in mine. "Are you hungry?" I ask to get my mind off touching her.

"Starved, actually. Who knew racing through the desert would burn so many calories?"

"It's the sun and the heat," I tell her. "When Ford and I were overseas, we could be sitting outside doing nothing, and I was probably hungrier than if we were actually working."

It's quiet for a few moments before she asks, "What was it like over there? Ford's never really said too much, probably to protect us, but I know he talked to my dad. Dad was no stranger to being sent away, which sucked for him and my mom. He missed us being born, and he'd had enough. Six months later he was home for good."

I can't help myself now. I reach over and grab her hand, holding hers within my much larger one and giving it a gentle squeeze. She slips her fingers through mine, entwining them as I've been picturing all day. The result causes my heart to simultaneously skip a beat with excitement and relax in contentment.

"I can't imagine growing up with a parent in the military like that. I'm the first one to enlist in my family. My grandpa had a childhood heart condition, which prevented him from enlisting, and by the time my dad was nearing the end of high school, he was helping full time with the farm. I think they always thought I'd hang around and join them, but I saw my future a little differently. I wanted to see more of the world and do my part to make it a better place before I put down roots somewhere."

"You're a good person, Chad Anthony. I'm super proud of you," she replies softly, squeezing my hand—and maybe my heart a little too.

"Anyway, being in Afghanistan is pretty much what you'd expect. It was hot during the summer months and at times, the hours were long and grueling. I remember feeling like everyone was watching me, and I guess they were. We were the Americans, coming into their towns and villages for whatever reason. For all the bad I saw—and believe me, there was plenty of that—there was a lot of good too. I have a ton of memories of playing soccer and hopscotch in the dirt streets with some of the kids and teaching a little girl how to tie her shoes. There's a lot of bad in the world, but there's a hell of a lot of good too."

"When I was in third grade, I remember our teacher's son being in the military and he was sent overseas somewhere. Every Friday, our class would write him a letter or draw him a picture. He was our pen pal, I guess you could say. Mrs. Winger would put together a package, sometimes a big box with snacks for him and those in his unit, and sometimes just a big envelope with that week's messages from the kids. She'd always write her own letter too and include it. A few times, we'd even be able to schedule video chats with him. I remember how excited everyone was, mostly because it was hard to picture a world so big that someone could be thousands of miles away and we could still communicate with them. On those days, we all were wearing our red, white, and blue, and he'd always smile so widely when we showed our support.

"One Monday, we were supposed to have a video chat, but Mrs. Winger wasn't there. The substitute told us there was an accident involving Brogan, her son, but wouldn't tell us anything more. Turns out, his Humvee hit a roadside bomb. All six inside were killed. Mrs. Winger never returned that school year, and it was my first real look at how dangerous military life really was. My parents never talked about it with us, and I can understand why. No one wants to tell their children their father could leave and never come back. That year changed how I viewed our military and those who serve."

My throat is tight as I try to swallow over the lump and absorb her words, the fear we face all too real.

"When Ford enlisted, I recall exactly how gripping that fear felt. I was transported right back to third grade, to the little girl who felt something so big, yet didn't really comprehend it until she was older. I have never been so terrified in my life than when he was gone. I constantly worried about him and if I would ever see him again."

I don't even realize I'm pulling the car over along the side of the deserted road until I'm stopping and throwing it in Park. Turning to face her, I see tears in those gorgeous emerald eyes. Tears that gut me right to the core.

Squeezing our joined hands once more, I bring the other up to her cheek and cup her soft skin. "I'm sorry you experienced that."

She gives me a watery grin. "That's life. The beauty and the pain. You can't have one without the other."

"Unfortunately," I agree, recalling all the heartache that has accompanied my time in the military. Like life in general, there has been a lot of good, but also plenty of bad too.

"Promise me something," she says, flashing me a sad smile.

"Anything."

"Promise me if you ever go, you'll be careful. I can't ask you to promise not to go, but you have to promise to do everything you can to come home at the end."

Her request has me reaching for her other hand. "Darlin', I promise I'll do everything in my power to come home," I reply softly, running my thumb across her knuckles. "If I could promise never to go away again, I would in a heartbeat, but that's not something I can guarantee."

Her lips turn upward, but her eyes reflect a lot of sadness with that single gesture. "I know, and I was teasing a little when I said that part. I'd never ask you to promise me that, honestly. I know there are no guarantees in this life, especially in the military."

"No, there's not," I concede, wishing I could take her in my arms and hold her close and never fucking let her go. "But I can promise I'll do everything in my power to come home at the end of the day. Even if I'm thousands of miles away. Okay?"

She nods and leans into my touch again, taking a deep breath and slowly exhaling. Her eyes close and the faintest smile plays across her lips. She looks so... content. And so fucking beautiful it hurts. Faith tilts her head just the slightest, her warm, soft lips resting against the inside of my thumb. She moves her mouth and kisses my hand. It's not a friendly kiss. That slightest touch is packed with passion, desire, and perhaps a hint of intent, and it goes straight to my balls.

Needing a change so I don't drag her into the back seat of the rental and maul her like a damn animal, I drop my hand to sever the connection. Her eyes slowly open as I ask, "Ready to get back so we can grab a bite to eat?"

Hurt and confusion flash in her eyes before it's pushed away. "Yes," she replies, that one word thick in her throat. She clears it away and sits up in her seat, adjusting the belt across her chest. It almost seems like she's giving her hands something to do.

I feel terrible.

I wanted to kiss her.

So fucking bad that the need caused physical pain, but when I kiss her, I'm not going to want to stop, so now isn't the time.

The drive back to Fort Irwin is comfortable, mostly because I never let go of her hand. We chat about everything. Her family, mine, my new job, and the base I now call home. I even explain The Box, part of the training process I have to do every couple of weeks, which is set to begin the Monday after she leaves.

"I have an idea," I say as we approach town and I head toward the hotel. "How about I drop you off so you can jump in the shower, then I'll run and pick up some food and meet you back in your room? Unless you want to go out somewhere. I can drop you off, run back to the barracks and shower, and be back in thirty."

"No, I think I'd prefer eating in."

I pull up in front of the hotel, flip on my hazard lights, and jump out. When I meet her around at the passenger door, she asks, "What are you doing?"

"Walking you up," I state, shutting the door and taking her hand.

"It's not far. I'm sure I can manage," she quips, her lips curling heavenward.

"You're more than capable, but there's no need to go alone if I'm able to be by your side." I don't realize how significant and true those words are until I've said them.

Faith doesn't argue. She walks beside me as we make our way through the small lobby of the hotel and to the elevator. We step inside, and within a few moments, are whisked away to the third floor. I don't release her hand until her room is unlocked and opened.

"What would you like for dinner?"

"Anything," she replies, turning to face me. "I'm not picky."

"What don't you like?"

She seems to take a few seconds to think before she replies, "I'm not a fan of roast beef dishes. You already know I prefer onion rings over french fries, and I don't like mustard on my hamburgers, but something else I could live without is German chocolate cake. Who wants to ruin chocolate with something as nasty as coconut pecan frosting?"

I lean forward and kiss her forehead. "Thank you. I'll be back in just a little bit. Lock up behind me," I state, turning and stepping back into the hallway. When she goes to shut the door, I add, "Oh, and, Faith? I hate mustard on my burger too." I toss her a smile and wink, then head for the elevator, making sure her door is secured before I step onto the car.

Jumping back in the rental, I make the short drive to the diner and place our order. "Give us ten minutes," the server says, placing our order with the kitchen.

"I'll be right back. I'm going to run an errand real fast," I tell her, making sure to give extra in the tip in case I'm a few minutes later.

"Not a problem, hon," she replies, already moving on to refill drinks for the customers at the counter.

I slip into the rental and make a quick trip to my barracks. After showing my ID, I park in the nearest lot and run to where my bed is.

"What are you doing back here? I thought you'd be out all night with your girl," Sanders says as soon as I enter the large room.

"I'm just grabbing a change of clothes," I tell him. When I decided on today's activities, I hadn't anticipated the sand. I should have stopped here and showered first, then went to place our food order. However, since I didn't think about that until after I paid for our to-go order, I'm lacking on options. Here's to hoping she's okay with me using her shower.

I throw an Army T-shirt, pair of athletic shorts, underwear, socks, and deodorant into a pile on my bed and grab my running shoes. Once I have what I need, I glance around the room. Besides Sanders, Howe and Harwood are here, playing a game of cards. "It's Saturday night. Don't you ladies have skirts to chase?" I tease.

"My wife doesn't approve of skirt chasing," Howe announces with a grin.

I stop and face the other newest member of the team. "You're married?"

He nods proudly. "Six months. I have my name on the list for married housing and was told it could be any day. There are several opening up. I'm anxious to get her here with me."

"I bet," I reply, grabbing all my stuff and heading for the door.

"With that group transferring out, there should be some apartments and small houses available early next week. I'm just waitin' for the call," he adds, tossing his cards onto the table as he folds.

I throw a wave over my shoulder and head out. When I reach my rental, I chuck my clothes into the passenger seat and jump behind the wheel. I stop at the security gate and do my thing there before making my way back to the diner to pick up our food. The entire trip only took fifteen minutes, so I'm only a handful of minutes behind to grab the order.

By the time I make it back to her room, I have my arms loaded with my clothes and bags of food, including two slices of homemade pie I bought on a whim before I left the diner. Using the spare key, I let myself into the room and find her standing in the bathroom wearing a tight tank top and tiny little shorts that barely cover her ass. Also known as her pajamas. I remember them vividly from our night together in a hotel room similar to this one over a year ago.

"Oh my goodness, that smells amazing," she says, running a brush through her wet hair.

"It's ready when you are. How was the shower?" I step farther into the room and set the bags down on the small table.

"Heaven. You should see all the sand in the bottom of the tub," she replies with a chuckle.

"I brought something for me to change into. Do you mind if I use your shower?" I holler, only to startle a moment later when she places her hand on my upper arm.

"I don't mind. Hell, it's practically your shower anyway, since you're paying for it."

"No, it's your space. I may be paying for it, but it's all for you," I insist, catching a whiff of her floral shampoo and bodywash.

Jasmine.

She leans in just enough that her tits brush against my arm. My dick is already hard, but now it's painfully so. Turning my head, I realize exactly how close she's standing, exactly how close her mouth is to mine.

Taking a step back, I put some much-needed air between us and reach for the bag of food. "Let's eat while it's still hot."

Between the two of us, we devour two cheeseburgers, an order of fries and onion rings, while watching the original *Batman* movie from the late eighties. I toss the containers back in the bag and set it beside the garbage can.

"I'm going to shower," I state, grabbing my clothes and trying not to notice how relaxed and amazing she looks spread across the bed.

"Okay," she replies, flashing me a smile.

When I'm alone in the shower, I contemplate taking care of my very eager cock. No way can I lie beside her on that bed and not want to touch her. Hell, I'll still want to touch her even if I take the edge off. I opt for just a quick wash—despite my dick really wanting a little attention—using her shampoo and bodywash, of course.

I slip on boxer briefs and athletic shorts, leaving my shirt off until my body cools down enough to stop sweating, thanks to the shitty ventilation system in the small bathroom, and step out into the main room. Faith is exactly where I left her, lying on the bed, and looking like a wet fucking dream.

My wet dream.

"The next *Batman* is on," she says, scooting forward, indicating there's plenty of room for me.

Shit.

Even though I know the right move would be to go sit in the chair, my legs carry me right toward her. Sliding onto the bed, I reach for her. Her slender body molds to me, my front to her back. It's too much—the pleasure she stirs inside me without even trying.

I grab the pillow and prop it under my head before resting my hand on her hip. If only I could ignore the heat of her skin beneath my fingertips.

After only a few minutes of watching *Batman Returns*, she whispers, "Chad?"

"Hmm?" I go ahead and lean forward just a bit and inhale the familiar scent of her intoxicating shampoo.

She seems a little nervous as she asks, "Can you stay tonight?"

"Yes," I reply instantly. This is exactly why I went ahead and applied for an overnight pass.

"Chad?"

I can't help but grin. "Yes, Faith?"

When she glances over her shoulder and meets my gaze, something hot and primal stirs to life in my gut.

"Will you kiss me?"

The smile falls from my face as I move toward her. I know I said I wasn't going to kiss her unless she was mine, but I just can't resist her. She's everything. "It'd be my pleasure."

My earlier words buzz through my mind. This only means one thing: Faith is mine.

She just doesn't know it yet.

I press my lips to hers, and finally—*finally*—all is right in the world again.

Chapter 6

Faith

EVERYTHING IN MY WORLD FADES AWAY. EVERYTHING BUT HIM. I never knew that it was possible for your world to feel as though it's tilting on its axis and righted at the same time. That's the result of his lips pressed to mine after all this time.

Asking him for this is wrong. We agreed that we would remain friends, and I've accepted that, but I also needed this from him. I need to feel the soft press of his lips, the warmth of his breath, and the taste of his tongue as it slides against mine.

I just needed him.

Chad.

He slows the kiss and rests his forehead against mine. He's breathing heavily, which keeps me from being self-conscious of the fact that I'm struggling to pull breath into my lungs. I don't know if it's more from the kiss or the man. I'm guessing a combination of both.

"I'm sorry." I finally find my words, pushing them past my lips.

"What are you sorry for?" He wraps an arm around me as he holds me close, pressing his lips to my forehead.

"I shouldn't have asked you to do that." I bite down on my bottom lip while moving my head to his bare chest. He runs his fingers through my hair, never wavering on the hold he has on me.

"Do you regret it?"

"No." A few heartbeats pass before I whisper, "Do you?" I hold my breath waiting for his reply. It comes immediately.

"Never."

"We said we were just friends." It's a reminder not only for him but for me as well.

"Friends can kiss." His facial expression gives nothing away. I don't know what he's thinking other than the fact that he seems to be defending our actions. I'll take that as a mark in the win column.

I lift my head so that I can look him in the eye. "Do you kiss all of your friends like that?"

"Like what?" Finally, there's a slight tilt to his lips, and I know he's messing with me.

"Like you need them to breathe?"

His eyes darken at my words, and I want to grin that I've shocked him and maybe even turned him on a little, but I contain it.

His heated expression simmers as his eyes soften. Lifting his hand, he pushes my hair back out of my eyes. "No. Just one. She's special."

Hot tears well behind my eyes, so I avert my gaze and rest my cheek back on his chest. He has no idea what his words do to me. I want to be special to him. I want to be his someone. I see what my brother and Shayne have, and I want a love like that. I want it with Chad, but that's not what we agreed to. He's in California, and I'm in Ohio. Two worlds, so close yet so far apart.

"She's beautiful. Dark brown hair and these big green eyes that could convince me to do anything she asked. She's a tiny little thing but full of fire and grace. And her name, well, it's a token of who she is. I know that I can trust her with my life. Maybe even someday, if all the stars align, with my heart too."

My heart races, and blood whooshes in my ears so loud I can't hear anything but the steady thrum. I snuggle in closer, and Chad, always knowing exactly what I need, holds me tighter. He wraps those strong arms around me, and I want to beg him to never let me go.

Finally, when I feel as though I have my emotions under control, I once again lift my head and find his eyes already there.

Watching. Waiting.

"She's you, Faith," he says, his voice low and gravelly. I nod, not able to speak. "Tell me what you need?" He runs the pad of his thumb beneath my eyes as if he knows I'm battling tears that threaten to fall.

I swallow hard. "You." My voice cracks. "More kisses, and for tonight, can we just... can we maybe pretend that we didn't make a choice all those months ago in that hotel room that has us keeping each other at arm's length? Can we pretend that you don't live a plane ride away from me?"

He rolls over to his side so that we're eye to eye. His body is aligned with mine, and his arms hold me close. "I'll be anything you need, Faith. Anything."

Mine.

"Kiss me," I murmur, closing my eyes. Not willing to witness the look in his eyes if he changes his mind. Only he doesn't change his mind as our lips connect. It's his warm, soft lips ghosting over mine. I settle into his embrace and allow myself to get lost in him. In his rough, calloused hands as they slide beneath my shirt and the way my leg finds itself snuggled in between his. The feel of his tongue exploring my mouth and the way my other hand is buried in my hair, holding me to him as if he's fearful I might disappear.

His hand slides up and slips beneath my bra strap. "Tell me to stop," he whispers against my lips.

"Don't stop."

Please don't ever stop.

He growls, and my entire body shivers as need races through me. "Faith." My name is a plea from his lips.

"Just for tonight," I counter. "Pretend with me. Just for tonight." I'm begging him to give me this. To give us this night. I don't know what it means, but I know I need more of him. More than just kisses. I want to feel his hands against my skin. I want to be able to explore him like I've dreamed of. I want him to explore me too. I just hope that he wants the same thing.

"I'm not strong enough to tell you no."

The look he gives me tells me he's not going to. He wants this. He wants me.

"Good." I smile as I kiss his jaw. "Just for tonight," I say, kissing toward his ear.

His grip on my hair tightens, not painful but enough for me to know he's struggling. When I feel the snap of my bra release and the whoosh of hot breath fan against my cheek, I know we're about to cross a line we've never crossed.

Outside of one incredible night. We've never taken things farther other than that one incredible night. He kissed the breath from my lungs until my lips were red and swollen. That same night, we decided to let whatever happens happen between us. Since then, it's been a lot of phone calls and video chats, and he'd visit when he could. When he was stationed in Kentucky, I made weekend trips when school would allow. We haven't kissed since that first night Shayne and I sent him and Ford back to base. We've hugged, held hands, and shown affection, but nothing like tonight.

Tonight changes things.

Tonight, I'm asking him to pretend the barrier we placed between us no longer exists. Tonight is also when I know with one-hundred-percent certainty, I'm in love with my best friend. I've known for a long damn time, but it's in this moment that I know there is no going back.

I love him.

"I need this off," he says, tugging at my shirt, bringing me back to the present. Dazed from his kisses, I manage to sit up and allow him to pull my shirt over my head before tossing it on the floor.

"Fuck, you're beautiful," he says as he slowly slides each strap of my bra over a shoulder, pulling it from my body and tossing it behind him, not giving a single fuck where it lands.

He's frozen as his eyes roam over parts of me he's never seen before.

"Chad?"

He jerks his head up to look me in the eyes. What I see would bring me to my knees if I weren't lying down.

I watch as his throat bobs as he swallows hard, finding his voice. "Can I touch you?"

Four words I've always wanted to hear from him.

"I don't know the rules here, Faith." He closes his eyes and furrows his brow. When he opens them, they're swirling with desire. He lifts his hand as if he's going to touch me, but instead, it hangs there suspended in the air between us. "Tell me." His voice is full of grit and need.

"I want you to touch me." I'm being bold, more so than I've ever been with him. I've always been afraid to tell him I want more, but not tonight. Tonight, I'm asking for it all. For as much as he'll give me, and even though I know there will be consequences, I'm willing to take them to get his hands all over me.

"Where?" he croaks.

This time it's me who's placing my hands against his cheeks. "Everywhere."

"Fuck," he curses but wastes no time reaching out and rolling a pert nipple between his thumb and forefinger. I close my eyes because

I just want to feel. I want to remember every touch. "Open your eyes for me."

I slowly blink them open to find him watching me.

"I need your eyes on me, baby."

I nod. Speaking anything coherent just isn't something I'm able to do at the moment.

Getting his other hand in on the action, he tests the weight of my breast in his palm, gliding his thumb across my pebbled peak. A moan falls from my lips, and he grins, satisfied that he's eliciting that sound from me.

His eyes find mine, and he holds my gaze. There are no words passed between us, but we don't seem to need them. He's asking me if I'm okay with this. He's asking if he's allowed to go farther, and my silent answer to both is yes. Finding the answer he needs, he dips his head and swipes his tongue across my hardened nipple, one and then the next.

I grip the sheets, holding myself still, not wanting to make a wrong move and have him pull away. I've thought of this moment more times than I care to admit, and now that it's happening, I don't want anything to ruin it for me.

For us.

Chad slides his hand behind my back and traces my spine while his lips capture mine. He kisses me with abandon, telling me with his mouth that he's in this with me. He leans forward, causing me to fall back on the mattress. I was still sitting from where he stripped my shirt and bra from me. He makes love to my mouth while those large, calloused hands of his roam over my body. We're both still wearing pants, and I curse the fact that we are. I should have stripped while he was in the shower to seduce him, but then again, I didn't see this night ending like this.

Then again, maybe, hopefully, we're just getting started.

Pulling away from my mouth, he trails kisses down my neck and to my chest. When he reaches my breasts again, he wastes no time pulling a hard nipple into his mouth. He's nipping, and sucking, and licking, and I've never been more turned on in my entire life. I rub my thighs together to quell the ache he's creating inside me.

From one breast to the next, he takes turns loving on me. My hands are buried in his hair, and all I can do is hold on for the ride. He has a singular focus, and that's to get his fill, and I'm not complaining. Other than the moans he's pulling from deep in my chest that escape my lips, I'm not saying a word. I'm too fearful he might break out of the lustful haze he's in and stop.

I don't want him to stop.

In fact, I'm mentally trying to devise a plan to make this happen every night for the rest of my stay. That is until he bites down a little harder on my right nipple, and pleasure rolls through me. I feel a rush of heat between my thighs. I feel my face flush at my body's response to his mouth on me.

"So responsive," he murmurs, moving back to my left breast.

Over and over again, he ravishes me with his mouth. The pressure starts to build, and I'm no longer embarrassed. Instead, I grip his hair harder, holding him to me. "Don't stop," I pant.

He does as I ask, not once taking a break. His mouth and his hands are driving me insane. I shift on the bed, but he's onto me. He moves so that he's nestled between my thighs. I can feel his hard cock through the thin fabric of my pajamas, and when he grinds his hips, that's all it takes. I shoot off like a rocket. "Chad!" I call his name as pleasure rolls through me.

He doesn't stop until my body falls to the mattress. Then, he still doesn't stop kissing me. His lips trail down my quivering belly before starting their journey back. He stops at each breast, giving them equal attention before his lips glide farther up my chest, kissing up my neck until finally, he reaches my lips.

He lifts his head to stare at me. His eyes roam over my face, my chest, and my belly. Every part of me that's exposed to him, he rakes his gaze over as if he needs to memorize my every feature. When his eyes come back to mine, his lips tilt in a smile. "That was the sexiest fucking thing I've ever seen."

"Somewhere in the back of my mind, I know that I should be embarrassed that I did… that, just from your mouth on my breasts, but honestly, I'm too turned on and too blissed out to care. I'm sure I'll freak out later."

"No. Never. Please, don't do that." He kisses me quickly. "I promise you that was the hottest sexual experience of my life. To date."

"Can we not talk about you and other people?" I say, rolling my eyes playfully.

"Hey." He's suddenly serious. He cradles my face in the palm of his hand and doesn't speak until he's sure he has my full attention. He doesn't realize that he always does. Always has since the moment I met him. "There is no one but you." He taps his temple with his index finger on his free hand. "Up here"—he moves his hand to tap his chest over his heart—"or in here. All I see is you."

I want so badly to believe him, but I know he's all worked up from what we just shared. "Can you stay? We said one night, and I'd really like to fall asleep with you." I bite down on my bottom lip, worried this night is about to end.

"Is that what you want? For me to stay?"

I nod. "I want you to hold me. Like that night."

I don't need to elaborate. He knows exactly what I'm talking about.

"Can I still kiss you?"

This pulls a smile out of me. "The night's not over."

"Do you happen to know how to freeze time?" he asks.

This time I laugh and swat playfully at his shoulder. "No, but if I did, I would have already done it."

He nods thoughtfully, letting me know he would have done the same.

"If only," he says, pressing his lips to my forehead.

"Chad?"

"Yeah?"

"Tell me this won't change us." Something passes in his eyes, but it's gone before I can name it.

"I give you my word."

I nod because that's good enough for me. Chad Anthony is honorable, and I know that anything he tells me is his truth.

"You ready for bed?" he asks.

"I... should probably go clean up."

His eyes flare with heat. I almost ask him to help me. Almost.

He goes to move, and I feel his hard length against my inner thigh.

"Let me." I reach for him, but he stops me placing his hand over my wrist.

"I'm okay."

"I want to."

"Faith." He sighs. "I want you to. Trust me, I want your hands on me, but I know me. I know there is no way I'm going to stop there. I need you too much right now."

"Let me."

He kisses me softly. "I'm okay, baby. Go clean up." He motions toward the bathroom.

I want to fight him on this. I want to demand he let me give him what he gave me—the best night of my life. But I also know once he's made up his mind, there is no changing it.

Besides, we've pushed the boundaries too far tonight already. I don't want to risk him or our friendship because I'm greedy.

Instead, I climb out of bed, grab his shirt that he never put on that's lying on the end of the bed, and rush to the bathroom, closing the door. I brace my hands on the counter and pull in a deep breath.

Lifting my head, I look in the mirror, and I don't recognize the woman staring back at me. My eyes are bright, my body is flushed, and my heart is full and cracked at the same time.

Tonight is one I will replay over and over and over again. When I'm lying in bed alone thinking about him, wondering what he's doing and if he's safe, tonight will help me through that. And if he gets deployed again, something I can't stand to think about, I can remind him of this night in my letters. I can remind him that if and when he's ready for more, that I'll be at home waiting for him with open arms.

I might even tell him that I'm irrevocably in love with him.

Chapter 7

Chad

I'M NOT QUITE SURE HOW I'M WIDE AWAKE ON MINIMAL SLEEP THE last two nights, but I am. It reminds me a bit of the excitement and nervousness of being overseas. Except this time, it's because there's the most amazing woman next to me.

In my arms.

Faith is sleeping soundly, her tiny body curled up against me. She fits so damn perfectly. The feel of her soft skin molded to mine has kept my mind busy for hours. Especially once she threw her bare leg over the top of mine, the heat of her pussy seeping through the silky panties pressed against my thigh. Every time I close my eyes, I see her coming. It's a vision and a sound I'm not likely to ever forget.

It's been torture to keep my hands idle when all they want to do is reach out and caress her softness. The few hours of sleep I was able to grab did nothing to calm the storm of desire brewing inside me, so it's been especially hard—pun intended—to just lie here and keep my hands to myself. Despite being the most content I've been in probably my entire life.

When the clock strikes six thirty, she stirs and reaches for me. Her hand slides down my chest and lands on my lower stomach, so very close to my throbbing erection. But I don't move. I don't make a sound. I just continue to count backward from one hundred, trying to will my cock into submission.

The fucker has a mind of his own though, especially with her hand... there.

The best thing for me to do is to get up and jump in the shower. I hate the thought of a jerk session in her space, but I'm not sure I'll be able to make it back to the base without some sort of serious damage to my family jewels. I'm not sure they've ever been this swollen and blue, including during my time as a horny teenager.

Before I can slip from the bed, her hand moves again. Those delicate fingers cup my erection, palming it in the most delicious way and applying gentle pressure. A muddled groan fills the room, one laced with the mixture of pain and pleasure I feel running through my veins.

"Chad?" Her sleepy voice breaks through the sex-fueled fog in my brain.

"Morning, sunshine," I reply, though it comes out a little gruffer than intended.

Her beautiful green eyes open and look up, meeting my gaze. I'm about to beg her to release my dick because he's about two seconds away from exploding, but all thought flees my big brain the moment she slips her hand beneath my shorts.

Her soft skin slides along my erection. "Fuck, Faith, you have to stop."

However, the little vixen does no such thing. "I don't want to stop. I don't think he wants me to stop either," she says coyly, wrapping her hand around my cock and giving him a gentle squeeze.

Nope. He definitely doesn't want her to stop.

"Faith," I groan in warning as she slides her palm up to the head. "I was just about to get up and take a shower."

She gently moves her hand down to the root of my cock, asking, "What were you going to do in the shower? This?" She strokes again, and my balls draw up with impending release.

"Yes," I bite out.

"That's silly, really. Especially when I'm more than capable of helping you out in your time of need."

And she does.

All I can do is reach for the pillow and hang on, because my orgasm is barreling down on me at Mach 10 speed. There's no stopping it now. I can't. The only thing left is to offer a warning. "I'm going to come, Faith."

Her wide green eyes are full of heat when she whispers, "Good, Chad. I want you to come. Now."

And I do.

Hard.

Probably harder than I ever have before. I can't even think about the force and the pain mixing with the pleasure as I release everything onto my stomach. I just feel. Feel how mind-blowing her warm, tight hand feels gripping me, milking my cock and every drop of cum from my body.

After a few seconds, she whispers, "You okay there, champ?"

"No," I groan, my brain too scrambled to come up with any other response.

Faith chuckles and shifts. "I'll grab a towel," she states, disappearing into the bathroom and returning a moment later with a hand towel. Once I have the mess on my stomach cleaned up, she asks, "What's the plan for today?"

I lift the blanket and pull her beneath it, directly against my body. "Well, I thought we could snuggle for a little while."

"Snuggle? Are big, bad military guys supposed to say snuggle?"

I reach down and poke her in the side, causing her to squirm and thrash. "Big, bad military guys can say whatever they want," I quip, curling my fingers into her soft skin and making her giggle.

"You're a big ol' softy," she teases, clearly enjoying razzing me a bit and causing me to tickle her more. "Stop!" she begs, wiggling and trying to pull away from me.

"Stop calling me a softy. There's nothing *soft* about me," I state, pivoting my hips forward and rubbing my sudden erection against her leg. I'm not sure how I'm hard so damn fast after coming, but it can only be attributed to her.

Faith.

I pull my fingers from her flesh and revel in the feel of her relaxing against me. "That wasn't nice," she mutters, clearly not upset with me for tickling her, since she's cuddling into my side once more.

"I'm sorry."

She snorts. "I don't think you are. You did that on purpose."

Smiling, I turn my head and kiss her forehead. "You're right. I did."

"It's okay. I'll get you back sometime," she says through a yawn.

"I'm not ticklish."

"Everyone's ticklish, Chad. I just have to find the right spot."

My dick twitches. "I might enjoy that."

She giggles the sweetest sound. "I bet you would." After a few long seconds of silence, she asks, "Do you think you can sleep?"

I'm surprised to realize I can. My entire body is relaxed and heavy, most definitely because of the relief I feel in my groin, thanks to the beauty beside me. "Yeah, I think I can," I state honestly, my eyelids growing heavy.

"Good. You didn't sleep much last night," she whispers, drawing her fingers across my bare chest and circling my right nipple.

"And how do you know that? You seemed to sleep well," I reply, resting my nose against her hair and inhaling.

I feel her shrug. "I seem to be very in tune to you."

I exhale and hold her close, my eyes automatically closing. "Likewise, beautiful. Likewise."

"Is that a hickey, Corporal Anthony?"

I instantly reach up and grab my neck. When I left Faith, it was with a short peck on the forehead, just as it has been the last few nights since I left her on Sunday to return to base. If I could have stayed Sunday, I would have, but my overnight weekend pass was only for Saturday. And while I can leave base during the evening throughout the week, I'm expected back to sleep. Leaving her each night has been difficult, so I just focus on the handful of hours we can steal together once I'm able to meet up with her again.

I live for those precious hours every day.

The guys around me start laughing, making me realize Sanchez was teasing me.

"You asshole," I state, throwing the workout glove I just took off at his head.

He ducks at the last second, my glove falling to the floor behind him. "Totally called it!" he announces to the others in the massive weight room before laughing and turning his attention back to the leg press machine.

"Just ignore him," Erik mutters beside me. "He's just jealous because he probably hasn't been laid since high school."

"Who said anything about getting laid?" I ask, arching a single eyebrow at the man beside me.

He flashes me a slightly smug, yet friendly grin. "I recognize the look of happiness," he states, adjusting the weights behind us.

Clearing my throat, I look away so he can't see my truth. The fact is I *am* happy. Happy with her here, and the thought of her leaving in a little over a week makes my stomach churn with uneasiness. She's barely been here five days, and I'm already hooked. Despite the fact he's a little off base with his "getting laid" assumption, he's spot-on when it comes to how I feel about Faith.

"Hey, thanks again for referring us to Hannah. Her appointment is this morning," I state, referring to his wife, who is going to treat Faith to a manicure and pedicure.

"Hannah's excited to meet her. She's slowly making friends here, thanks to working at the salon, but it can be hard when you know absolutely no one," Erik replies, getting into position on the bench.

I think about Faith and what it would be like if she were here. She has such an amazingly fun and energetic personality, I can see her making friends easily. From what I've heard and seen, kids love her, and I know she'll be an exceptional, caring kindergarten teacher when the opportunity arises.

"If you guys don't have anything planned Friday night, we can do that dinner we discussed," Erik says between reps of ten.

"I had mentioned it to Faith and she seemed up for it. I'll make sure Friday night is good with her, but I don't think we have any other plans," I reply, already thinking about taking her to dinner. I can't wait to hear how all her pampering appointments went today.

Realizing the time, I run through our checklist of stuff to do today. First, we have our team workout, followed by a five-mile run. Running doesn't usually bother me, but I'm not used to this desert dry heat yet, so I tend to dread them a little more than I used to. After the run, we'll shower and hit the mess hall before our training exercises this afternoon. It'll be a long, grueling day, but worth it. Not that I anticipate being called out anytime soon, but I suppose you never know. We're supposed to be here for two years, but if there's one thing I've learned during my time in the Army, it's to expect the unexpected.

"Just let me know after you talk to her tonight. If it won't work, that's okay. Don't feel obligated. I know she's only here for a short time, so if you don't want to share her with us, I get it. I did the same thing whenever Hannah would come for a visit."

"How'd that go for you guys?" I ask, genuinely interested.

"We started dating in high school. She went to a cosmetology school in Indiana, while I enlisted. I didn't know how it would work out, being apart like we were, but we were both committed. We talked on the phone or video chatted whenever we could and were always counting down the days until we'd see each other in person again."

His smile is far off as he looks over my shoulder. "The visits were great, but torture at the same time because I knew there was always a looming deadline. Saying goodbye sucked, and a few times, I thought about breaking it off with her. Not because I didn't love her or miss her like crazy, but because I felt like she was missing something in life by waiting around for me, and I didn't want that. Hannah always seemed to know when I was feeling particularly low and would reassure me, she was in this for the long haul.

"The day she graduated, I proposed. Best decision I ever made," he states proudly with a beaming smile.

I can't help but think about my own life and how Faith fits into it.

While Erik might have continued to date Hannah during their separation, I haven't dated Faith. Not because I didn't want to, but because I felt like she deserved better. No one should be sitting by the phone, waiting for a phone call. Not at our age. We're too young for that. And dating a military guy isn't easy. I've heard all the horror stories from guys and girls in previous units. It takes a strong person to commit to someone they barely see. Too many of them were cheated on, and I always vowed to never put myself or the woman I was seeing in that kind of situation.

Not that I think Faith would do anything like that, but I've spent a lot of time keeping women at arm's length. Especially after seeing the bullshit Ford went through with Sara. Ford and I met in boot camp and became fast friends. We were fortunate to be stationed together afterward and sent overseas at the same time. He told me a lot about the crap that happened when he enlisted. It had always been his plan, which she apparently knew. Yet somehow, she thought she could talk him out of it and blamed him for leading her on when her plan didn't work. He was messed up for a while.

Until he met Shayne.

Call me Cupid, because it was my invitation for him to come home with me for a week during leave, which resulted in him meeting Shayne. And the rest, as they say, is history. They're engaged to be married, living in their dream house, and are living happily ever after.

That's also how I met Faith. I'd heard all about her over the three years Ford and I were friends before I finally got to meet her. From the moment I saw her, I knew she was special. Different from any woman I had ever met before.

And I knew almost instantly, if we could overcome a little distance and time, we could have something great. I've felt it in my heart since that first night and every night after. Having her here is a blessing and a curse, because it's a reminder that I'm going to have to let her go again.

Soon.

"You good there, Corp?" Erik asks, pulling me out of my own head.

"Yeah, why?" I ask, getting into position to spot his next ten reps.

He just grins. "You just had a serious look on your face with a cheesy grin," he teases, clearly knowing where my mind had wandered.

"I was thinking about all the running I'm going to make you do once we're done here."

Erik laughs and reaches for the bar. "Sure you were," he quips, before lifting the bar and pounding out ten bench presses.

We switch places and I do the same, only with a little more weight. Erik might be a few inches taller than me, but he's a little on the leaner side. Don't get me wrong, he's strong as fuck, and I'd trust him to carry my ass out of any situation that arose without breaking a sweat. I feel the same about most of the guys in my new unit. Sure, there's still a couple I'm on the fence about, but for the most part, these are good teammates and soldiers.

That brings my mind back around to Faith. Ever since we met, she's been my biggest cheerleader and close friend. Yes, I still consider her twin brother my best friend, but there's something different about talking to Faith. We're connected on a deeper level; one I suspect is reserved for the one you love forever.

Do I love Faith?

Yes, of course I do. She's the most beautiful woman I've ever known, inside and out. She's caring, witty, and kind, which is why I know she's destined for great things as a kindergarten teacher. Even though the amount of time we've physically seen each other face-to-face is small, I've gotten to know the real her through hours and hours of phone, text, and video conversations over the last year.

Wherever I was, she was there too. In my head and my heart, right there beside me, even when she wasn't.

Clearing my throat, I push away all the emotions Faith brings to the surface. Now isn't the time to get into all that.

"All right, fellas. It's time to get ready for our run," I announce, grabbing everyone's attention and getting a mix of groans in return. No one particularly likes running in this kind of heat, but it's necessary. "Rehydrate and meet outside in fifteen."

I chug the bottle of water I brought and toss it in the trash.

Time to put thoughts about Faith aside and get back to work.

Chapter 8

Faith

THE GPS ON MY PHONE TAKES ME STRAIGHT TO THE HEALING Hands Day Spa. I can't keep the smile off my face when I think about Chad setting this up for me. He's making it harder and harder not to fall even more in love with him.

I'm already dreading next week when I have to get on that plane and head back to Ohio. At home, I'm uneasy and confused about the future. When I'm here with him, none of that holds the same level of concern. When I'm with him, everything else pales in comparison. It will all work out. It always does. I just wish I had that mindset when I'm thousands of miles away from him.

I grab the keys from the ignition of the rental, something else he did to make sure I was taken care of. My purse sits on the passenger seat, where I snatch it up, toss my phone inside, and climb out of the car.

The spa is a renovated house. It's a two-story Victorian home with a wraparound porch. Making my way up the steps, I pull open the door and step inside. I don't know what I was expecting, but it wasn't to feel as though I was stepping into a family home. It instantly puts me at ease. I can admit that I was a little nervous. I'm not an extravagant kind of girl, and spa day screamed fancy and expensive in my mind.

However, this place is casual, and I can get behind a mani, pedi, and massage. It feels like home, which is odd in so many ways, but I don't really know any other way to describe it.

"Welcome to Healing Hands Day Spa. How can I help you?"

"I'm actually looking for Hannah," I tell the woman behind the counter.

"I'm Hannah. You must be Faith."

"Yes. Hi." I wave awkwardly. She surprises me when she steps out from around the counter and pulls me into a hug.

"Welcome. I'm so glad you're here. I've been given strict instructions for you to spare no expense today."

I laugh nervously. "I'm not sure what that entails exactly, but I'm in," I tell her.

"That's what I like to hear." She gives me a genuine smile that has me taking a deep breath and dropping my tense shoulders. "Erik gave your Chad my number, and he made it abundantly clear that he wanted you spoiled today."

"He's not mine. I mean, we're not together. We're just friends," I ramble.

"You sure about that?" She raises her eyebrow in question. "No man has ever done this for someone who is just his friend. He was adamant that you have the full treatment."

"That's just Chad. He's a great guy, and he knows that I've been stressing about finding a job, and he feels guilty that he can't take time off to visit with me while I'm here."

Hannah grins, pointing a long-manicured nail at me. "There's a story there, and luckily we have all day to get to it."

"There's not much to tell."

"Uh-huh." She gives me a saucy grin. "How about we start with a pedicure? I have a client coming in for a haircut, but he's quick, and then the rest of the day, you get my full attention." She points to a pedicure chair. "I'll get you all set up to soak while I take care of him."

"Sounds good to me. I've got nowhere to be." I follow her to the line of pedicure chairs and take a seat. She gets the water going and offers me a drink before she rushes to cut the hair of her next client.

Sticking my feet into the warm water, I sigh as the massaging jet hits my arches.

How did Chad know this was exactly what I needed? Reaching into my purse, I pull out my phone and begin to scroll through social media. I'm worried if I don't keep my mind occupied, I might fall asleep in the chair, and the last thing that I want to do is embarrass myself or Chad like that.

I'm mindlessly scrolling when my eyes scan an ad. I sit up straighter in my chair. It's a job ad for a kindergarten teacher.

Finally!

Not willing to waste any time, I click on the link and quickly go through the process of applying for the position. I only hope that if they call me for an interview, it's not before I head back home. I don't want to leave Chad early. I crave this time with him, but I'll do what I have to do to get my dream job.

Luckily for me, I have my resume saved in the files on my phone, so I make quick work of filling out the online application and attaching my resume. Once I click Submit, I toss my phone in my bag, feeling an odd sense of relief. This is what I've been waiting for. Suddenly, my already amazing day just got a whole lot better.

Relaxing back into the chair, I allow myself to close my eyes, and with that, the tension fades away. I have a good feeling about this one.

"Ready?" Hannah asks, taking a seat on the stool and pulling one foot from the water. We make small talk while she starts on my pedicure.

"So, what's up with you and Chad?" She smiles at me, and it's one of those friendly smiles. The kind that instantly puts you at ease and has you wanting to spill your entire life story. Yeah, it was one of those, and that's why I open my mouth and start from the beginning.

By the time my story ends, she's sliding back on her stool and pointing for me to move to the table for my manicure. "You know he's in love with you, right?" she asks, taking her place behind the desk. "Are you doing your nails the same color as your toes?"

I look down at the deep sparkly purple color. "Yes." Then her previous words register. "I know that he loves me. That's not the issue. It's that he's not *in* love with me."

Hannah tosses her head back in laughter. "I disagree. Look, I've never seen the two of you together. I don't know how he looks at you or even if his eyes follow you no matter where you are in the room. However"—she holds up her hand when I start to reply—"I do know that he was insistent that this day be anything and everything you could want."

"He's a nice guy. One of the best," I add.

"Agreed. He's also in love with you."

"Oh, how I wish that were true."

"He stayed with you all weekend, and it wasn't just a friendly visit," she reminds me.

Yeah, I might have spilled it all. I needed someone to talk to, and Shayne's not here, and even if she were, she's too close to both of us. Hannah was the better option; that is until she started putting ideas in my head about Chad being in love with me.

A girl can dream.

"Erik said he invited you two to our place for dinner tomorrow night, right? Let me see for myself if my suspicions are correct."

"He's my best friend." I feel like a broken record.

She gives me a wide grin. "The best romantic relationships start from friendship."

"You'll see. It's friendship. Nothing more," I tell her with a light chuckle. I'm not convinced, but my heart is begging for her to be right. I'd give anything for Chad to be in love with me.

Pulling into the lot of the hotel, I don't even have to look into the rearview mirror to know I'm smiling. Today was a great day. I feel refreshed and completely pampered. I stopped at the local pharmacy and picked up some lotions. My plan is after we grab something to eat that, I will bring Chad back here and give him a massage. It's not even close to the day that he treated me to, but it's a start to say thank you.

Grabbing the bag and my purse from the passenger seat, I head up to my room. As soon as I swipe the key card and push open the door, I see him. Chad is lying on the bed, feet hanging off the side, hands crossed at his chest, and he's sound asleep. I know that my being here is catching up with him. He's usually back in his room and sound asleep well before curfew.

Quietly, so I don't wake him, I place both bags on the small table and move to his side of the bed. I don't know how, but I manage to take off both of his shoes and lift his legs to the bed without him stirring. Kicking off my own shoes, I move to the other side and climb in next to him. I move close, seeking his warmth. I lay my head on the pillow next to his and close my eyes. Just as I'm about to let sleep pull me under, he rolls to his side and pulls me into him. I settle in his arms, not sure if he's sleeping or if he's awake. I just enjoy the fact that I'm here and try not to think about leaving next week.

I could stay right here every day of forever.

I feel his lips press to my forehead and whisper, "Missed you."

Lifting my head, I find his tired eyes on me. "I missed you too."

"How was your day?" He rolls onto his back, taking me with him, so I'm now lying on his chest.

"It was everything I didn't know that I needed. Thank you. Hannah is so sweet, and we hit it off right away. I'm really excited for dinner on Friday."

He smiles. It's lazy and happy and has my heart tripping over in my chest. "I know I just met them too, but they seem like good people."

"I'm excited to go. Unless you changed your mind and made other plans for us?"

"No. No other plans. Just spending every second I don't have to be on base with you."

If he only knew how his words affected me. Can he hear the thunderous beat of my heart? "Are you hungry?"

"Starving."

"How about we stay in? We can order pizza."

"I should take you out."

"I've been out all day, and you're exhausted. We can eat now, and you can head back to base early and get some rest."

"No. I'm not leaving you until I absolutely have to. You came all this way to spend time with me, and that's what's going to happen."

"So bossy," I tease.

"I don't want to miss a minute, Faith." He tightens his hold on me, and my heart melts.

"Okay. I just don't want you wearing yourself out just because I'm here."

"I'm good. I got a quick nap, and now I want to hear about your day."

"Let me order pizza." I roll out of his arms and off the bed, making him laugh. I go to my purse on the table to get my phone. "I got something for you today," I tell him as I pick up the flyer on the TV stand for the local pizza delivery.

"Did you get me you?" he asks.

I look over my shoulder at him and see he's staring at my ass. "Do you want me?" I ask. My eyes widen when I realize what I asked. "I mean do you want it to be me?" Shit, that's not much better. With my face flushed, I turn back around and dial the number, placing the phone to my ear.

The call connects instantly, and I order us a large pizza, some boneless wings, and bread sticks. I figure Chad can take whatever we don't eat back to the barracks for later or to share with the guys. Not to mention, I know he can put away food, especially after the long physical days he puts in. I rattle off my room number and drop my phone on the table, and that's when I feel his hands on my hips.

He kisses my neck, running his lips up to my ear. "I want you, Faith. I want it to be you. The answer to both of your questions is yes. Always yes."

I turn in his arms and wrap my own around his waist, burying my face in his chest. I need a minute to get my emotions under control. I don't know how I'm going to be able to get on that plane next week. My heart physically aches at the thought of being away from him.

"Go sit on the bed. Shirt off."

"Now we're talking." He smacks a loud kiss on my lips and moves toward the bed, reaching behind his neck, tugging off his plain black T-shirt, and tossing it on the chair in the corner of the room.

I make quick work of pulling some cash out of my wallet and laying it on the table before grabbing the bottle of lotion from the bag. I crawl onto the bed and settle behind him. My legs are wrapped around him, where he sits on the edge of the bed.

"This might be cold," I tell him.

His hands grip my thighs as he pulls me close. My front is molded to his back. "I can't do what I had planned sitting that close." I laugh and try to scoot back, but his grip on my thighs is too tight.

"I want you close."

"You're messing with my mojo, mister."

"Am I supposed to say I'm sorry? You're not going to get that from me."

I lightly smack his shoulder. "Humor me."

"Humor me," he fires back, giving my thighs a gentle squeeze.

"Fine. This is going to be a quick few passes until the pizza gets here anyway. After we eat, I'll make you lay down on the bed, so I can get a better angle on it."

"I don't know what you're talking about, but I think I like it." He chuckles.

I pump some lotion into my palm before rubbing my hands together to warm up the lotion. When my hands land on his shoulders and I begin to knead at his stiff muscles, he moans, dropping his chin to his chest.

"Damn," he mutters.

"You're tight."

"So are you."

Again, I playfully swat at his back. "What has gotten into you tonight?"

"You. I love that you're here, Faith. I love knowing that after a long, hard, grueling day, I get to be here with you. Like this." He turns to look at me over his shoulder, and on instinct, I lean in and softly press my lips to his.

"Thank you for bringing me out here."

He nods before turning back around. His hands are still gripping my thighs. He's not letting go, and that's perfectly fine by me. I don't want him to let go.

"How did you know I needed this today?" he asks.

"Because I didn't realize I did until Hannah got her hands on me earlier. Thank you again for that. Today was very relaxing."

"You're welcome."

"Oh, and I didn't tell you what else happened."

At the excitement in my voice, he turns his body so that he can see me. "Your eyes are sparkling."

"I'm excited. I was scrolling through my phone and saw an ad for a kindergarten teacher. I have my resume on my phone, so I applied right away."

"Seriously? Faith, that's incredible."

"I feel good about it. I haven't even spoken to them, but something in my gut tells me this job is going to be my future."

I'm shocked when he slides his hand behind my neck and pulls me into a tender kiss. "I love this for you. I'm sending all the good vibes to the universe for you to get your dream job," he says, pulling away from the kiss.

Before I can reply, there's a knock at the door. I scramble off the bed and rush to the money I already have laid out. Chad reaches for my arm, but I sprint for the door, tugging it open and thrusting the cash at the delivery guy. The teenager appears to be amused at the big man behind me who's whining he wanted to pay for dinner.

"Thank you," I tell the kid, taking our food and kicking the door closed. "My treat, handsome."

"What am I going to do with you?" He follows me to the table where we spread out. "I'm going to run to the vending machine and grab us some drinks."

"No need. I filled up the mini fridge earlier. I had some time before my appointment."

He leans over the table and kisses me. His tongue lazily slides against mine. "Thank you."

I nod because words fail me. This man is everything to me. I hear Hannah's voice in my head, and I can't help but wonder if she's right.

Can I risk telling him how I really feel?

I quickly shake out of that thought. Nothing is worth the risk of losing Chad as a part of my life.

Chapter 9

Chad

ER HANDS, THEY'RE FUCKING MAGIC. LIKE THE KIND OF hands you want touching you forever. Or maybe that's how I'm looking at them. Perhaps it's wishful thinking, that I'll be lucky enough to always have them on my body.

After we ate pizza, she insisted on finishing her massage. It wasn't necessary, but now that she's straddling my lower back and kneading the knots in my shoulders, I'm damn glad she was so persistent. This is heaven.

Soft music plays from her phone. At first, I thought it was a little cheesy, even though I went along with it, but now that we're in the moment, I definitely think the music is a nice touch. I feel more relaxed than I expected.

She slowly moves down, digging her fingers and the heels of her hands into my flesh. I can't help but moan.

"Is that a good moan or a bad one?"

"Good. Definitely good," I mumble, my face pressed into the mattress.

She spends a good half hour working out the kinks and tight muscles in my back, neck, and shoulders. The massage is great, but just having her hands on me is the icing on the cake. Especially when she's working on my neck and leaning forward, her tits brushing against my bare skin. Sure, she has her shirt on, but still. I can feel the swell of them with each move she makes, and it's not helping the stiffness in my pants.

"What do you think?" she asks, her movements slowing and the pressure from her touch subsiding.

"I think I'm never letting you go."

Her hands stop, and she doesn't say a word. I wonder if I said too much and risk a quick glance back. Her eyes are soft and locked on me as her fingers curl into my flesh. Without thinking about what's happening below the belt, I turn around, a task that's challenging, considering she's sitting on me. But Faith lifts herself enough to allow me to move, and the moment I'm flat on my back, she returns to straddling me.

Only this time, she's straddling my very hard cock.

Those sexy green eyes seem to darken before my own eyes, and her breathing comes out in little pants of excitement. My hands automatically move to her hips, sliding around to rest on the globes of her ass. My grip tightens just a touch as she rocks her hips. I can feel the heat from her pussy right where I want it, even if there are layers of clothes between us.

"Chad?" she asks, her eyes wide with anticipation.

"Yes, love?"

She swallows hard before asking, "Can I kiss you?"

"You never have to ask," I state, my throat dry and scratchy.

Faith leans forward and brushes her lips across mine. I try to keep my hands still, but they itch to touch her smooth, soft skin, and slowly move beneath her top to her lower back. The most satisfying mewl slips from her mouth as her tongue glides against mine. She tastes like pure heaven, all honey sweet and ripe.

She rocks her hips, grinding against my erection and whimpers. I have to stifle the groan, refusing to let my own pleasure take control of the situation. As much as I want to strip us naked and bury myself inside her, I won't push it. Sex will happen if and when she says it can, so I will grapple for every ounce of control I possess until she gives me the green light.

"I..." she murmurs against my lips.

"What?" I ask, sliding one hand into her hair and resting the other on her hip.

She gazes down at me, her hair falling in waves around her beautiful face. "I don't think I'm quite ready for..."

"That's fine," I insist when she's unable to get the words out. "We don't have to. I like kissing you."

A gentle grin spreads across her plump lips. "I like that too. And for the record, we can do... *other* stuff."

My own smile is wolfish as I gaze up at her. "What kind of *other* stuff are you thinking?"

There's a faint blush on her cheeks, and I'm not sure if it's from the words she's about to say or the fact she's turned on. "Well, I wouldn't mind getting my mouth on you."

Yes! Best idea ever.

"Funny, I was just thinking the same thing," I insist, running my hand around to her ass and squeezing. Lifting her up, we carefully sit upright and scramble from the bed. "Clothes. Off. Now."

She does as instructed while I do the same. We watch each other move, fingers and hands pulling at clothing until there's not a stitch left on either of us. We're both left naked for the very first time, and all I can do is stare in wonder.

She's breathtaking. Perfect.

Mine.

Her skin is so fucking soft as her arms wrap around my neck. Her tits press firmly against my chest, her nails digging into my scalp as our mouths meet once more. Our tongues battle, and I know I'll never get enough of her. She's everything I didn't even know I needed in my life, and the thought of not having her at my side is like a punch to the chest. The worst kind of torture. I need her.

Now.

And every day that follows.

Pushing thoughts of days not filled with Faith from my mind, I drop to my knees in front of her and lift her left leg. I rest it over my shoulder and grab her ass firmly. "Fuck, I can smell how badly you want this," I murmur, running my nose across the thin strip of hair above her pussy. "I can't wait to taste you."

She mumbles something and drives her fingers into my hair, holding me in place.

I pause long enough to look up and meet her gaze. "You sure?"

Her mouth is open, and she nods insistently. "I'm sure."

That's all I need to hear.

Moving forward, I take one long taste of her pussy, instantly needing more. I swipe my tongue across her clit, feeling her body tense by that one action. She tastes like heaven. Like a cool drink of water on a hot summer day.

And I'm very thirsty.

With my tongue, I draw pleasure from her body. I alternate between flicking her clit and sliding it inside her warm, wet heat. Of course, my body is so taut and tense, my cock begging for a little attention too, but that can wait. Right now, I'm going to savor this moment and having my mouth on her.

When her leg starts to shake, I realize we need a little change in positioning. "I have an idea," I tell her as I look up and meet her lust-drunk gaze.

"Does it involve you sliding your cock in my mouth?" she asks, the corner of her lips curling up in a naughty grin.

Standing up, I press my lips to hers chastely. "As a matter of fact, it does." When she doesn't pull away at the taste of herself on my tongue, I deepen the kiss.

Before we can get too carried away, I pull back and move toward the bed. I lie flat in the middle and give her a big smile. "Come here, love. Come straddle my face."

Her eyes darken even more as she climbs onto the bed and approaches my head. "Are you sure?"

My eyes are hard and insistent as I reply, "Fuck, yes, Faith. Get up here and sit on me."

She scurries, lifting her leg up and over my face. She's too far away for my tongue to reach her, so I gently place my palms against her thighs and pull down. My mouth meets her wet, swollen flesh, and my tongue delves deep inside her pussy.

Faith groans, swirling her hips around and seeking that glorious friction. Then, she leans forward, her tits falling against my stomach as she wraps her hand around my cock. Now it's my turn to moan. She draws my dick between her lips and lets it slide past her tongue into her throat.

"Christ," I grumble, trying to keep my bearings as she continues to suck me deep into her mouth.

"Mmm," she hums, the vibration going straight to my balls.

Refusing to let this end with a happy ending for me and not her, I place my hands on her ass and pull her down tightly against my face. I lick and suck her clit, reveling in how she squirms above me. She grinds down, searching for the sweet relief I dangle in front of her like a carrot.

I try to ignore how amazing her mouth feels, blowing my cock, but it's hard. *No pun intended.* All I want to do is get lost in the sensation, in the pleasure, and it takes all my strength to keep my focus where it should be—on her. So, when her pussy starts to contract around me, her arousal seeping around my face, I know she's getting close. I thrust my tongue inside her repeatedly, loving the tightness around me. My palms stroke the globes of her ass as I hold her in place. I let my fingers dance between her cheeks and graze across her puckered hole. At the intimate touch, I feel her entire body tense. I'm ready to apologize for touching her *there*, but there's no time. Faith detonates, coming hard above me.

She rocks her hips as she cries out, grinding her pussy against my face. But it's when she sucks my cock—hard—into her mouth that has me ready to blow right along with her. She moves frantically, her pace determined, as she holds my dick and sucks. When the head of my cock hits the back of her throat, I erupt, not able to give her a warning. She doesn't seem deterred in the slightest, just swallows every last drop I have until we're both boneless and breathless.

I place a kiss against her thigh. "Fuck," I mumble, trying to breathe normally but unable to do so.

"Mmm." She sighs contently, resting her face against my thigh. "I think we should do that again," she says through a yawn.

Chuckling, I roll her to the side and shift so we're face-to-face once more. "I'm not opposed to that, but I might need more than a couple of minutes. I think you sucked the life out of me," I quip, even though it's not far off base.

She gives me the sleepiest, sweetest smile that makes my heart lurch in my chest. "That was my plan."

I lean forward and place a kiss on her forehead. As much as I hate it, I need to head back to base. "I don't want to go," I say, realizing how very true that statement is.

Her eyes crack open as she sighs. "I know."

"What do you want to do about tomorrow night?"

She yawns again and closes her eyes. "I think we should go. It'll be fun."

"I agree," I tell her, slowly climbing from the bed and reaching for my discarded clothes. "How about I pick you up at five?"

"Okay," she mumbles, turning her face into the rumpled bedding.

My eyes are glued to her naked body as I dress, and when I have my shoes on my feet, I make my way to where she lies. "Come on, love, let's get you into bed," I murmur. Carefully, I lift her from the bed and turn her around, crawling onto the bed to place her head on the pillow. When she's in position, I pull the bedding over her body and bend down to kiss her lips. "Night, sweetheart. I'll see you tomorrow."

"Thank you for today, Chad. I had the best day," she whispers, giving me a second kiss.

"You're very welcome," I reply, making sure she's tucked securely beneath the covers.

I head for the door, turning off the lamp as I go and bathing the room in darkness. The last thing I see before slipping out the door is the most beautiful woman in the world. She owns my heart and doesn't even know it.

Maybe someday I'll have the balls to tell her how I really feel. Being with a military man is hard, and I'm too weak and selfish to let her go the way I should. I want to hang on, even if I don't deserve her.

One more week. I have one more week of her here, and then I'll let her go. Back to her life, where we're both tucked safely in the friend-zone. The one I dread but know is the right spot regardless.

Until then, I'll hold her close like the selfish bastard I am.

I'll always love her from afar, wishing things could have been different.

With Faith's hand tucked securely into my right one, I lift my left arm and knock on Erik and Hannah's door.

"Come in," Hannah greets, opening the door to their small house in the middle of the dozens of identical others, which makes up the married housing on base.

"Hey," Erik says, stepping behind his wife and offering a smile. "Welcome."

"We brought wine," Faith announces, giving Hannah the bottle after accepting a friendly hug.

"Oh, thank you. Let's go open it, shall we?" To her husband, she asks, "Can you check the grill?"

Erik leans forward and kisses her forehead. "Of course." When the ladies walk off, he hits me in the stomach and says, "Let's go."

I follow him as we move through the small house and step out onto the back patio. I can see other identical patios around us, some with grills and patio furniture, while others are empty. "So this is the marital housing, huh?"

Erik smiles, lifting the grill and checking the steaks. "Only another minute and these'll be ready. And, yeah, this is it. They're nothing fancy, but it sure beats the hell out of living in the bunkhouses at the base," he states, elbowing me in the gut.

I snort, mostly because he's right. "I have my name on the list, but they say it'll be a while before any open up."

"Too bad you're not married. There are a few of these places available, but I know there are rules."

I nod, understanding them but hating them all the same, mostly because I wish I had a place I could come home to every night. One where Faith is there and doesn't require us to part ways before curfew. "How's it going for you two? You haven't been married too long, right?"

He flips the steaks and closes the lid. "No, not too long, and I'm damn glad I did it. Not just because she's the best part of my life, but also because I know she'll be taken care of if something happens to me."

"What do you mean?" I ask as he grabs the platter to remove the meat.

He pauses, glancing my way. "Well, you know as well as I do that our jobs are dangerous. We could be called out at any time for God knows how long or where, and since we're married, I know she'll be taken care of. If something happens to me."

It's that last part that has me swallowing hard. It's not something military personnel talk about openly, but that doesn't mean it's not something we haven't thought about.

Even me, who has no significant other. I've thought about my parents, my friends and family.

Faith.

What would happen to her if something happened to me? Not that she's not capable of taking care of herself—she's more than capable—but... what if?

"That's part of the reason we got married so quickly," he tells me as he pulls four juicy steaks off the grill and places them on the platter. "Don't get me wrong, I was going to marry her anyway, but when I was sent here, we decided to do it sooner rather than later. I wanted to know my girl was taken care of, receiving all of my military benefits, you know?"

I nod and follow him back into the house where Faith and Hannah are waiting, sipping on wine. "This looks amazing, Hannah," I tell her as we join them at the dinner table.

"Thank you. I'm so glad you two were able to join us. I'm still meeting others around the base and am grateful to get to know you both," she replies with an open smile.

"Faith, I hope you like your steak medium-well," Erik says as he places slabs of beef on each of our plates.

"That's perfect," she replies, taking a helping of mashed potatoes before passing them along.

Everything smells amazing and my stomach starts to growl as my phone rings. I want to ignore it, ready to dive into the delicious food, but know I can't let it go to voicemail. "Hello?" I ask, instantly on alert as I listen to the caller.

I don't even know when I stood up, but by the time the call is over,

I have three sets of eyes staring back at me. Erik is on high alert, standing across from me at the table, his entire body tense. "Shit," I mutter, trying to process what I was just told.

"What?" he asks, his gaze intense and focused.

With a deep breath, I look at my teammate and friend and announce, "We're being sent out. We have until Wednesday morning at 0600, and then we ship to an undisclosed location."

I hear Hannah gasp, but my eyes zero in on the woman sitting beside me. Faith's eyes are wide with fear and sadness, and all I want to do is wrap her in my arms and shield her from the pain and worry I know she's experiencing.

The meal is forgotten as Erik consoles his crying wife. Faith stands up and reaches for my hand, and there's no missing the tears swimming in her eyes. Just the feel of her skin against mine brings a sense of calm I wasn't expecting. The world is at war around us—literally, it appears—and as long as I have her by my side, I know I can get through anything.

But can I ask her to wait for me?

While I'm gone to God knows where for God knows how long?

I want to.

Fuck, I want to so badly, I can taste it.

As I wrap my arms around Faith and her body molds perfectly to mine, I think back to what Erik said and an idea takes shape. It might not be the best idea in the world, but now that the seed is planted, I can't stop it from taking root in my mind. I spin the options around, trying to figure out a better way, but I'm not sure there is one.

If I want to protect her, this may be the only way.

I just have to make her see.

We need to get married.

Fast.

Chapter 10

Faith

MY HEART HURTS.

The ache in my chest refuses to go away. The pain was instant as soon as Chad said those four words. *We're being sent out.* I can still hear the agony in his voice.

How we all managed to compose ourselves to finish dinner, I'll never know. After a tearful goodbye, Chad drove us back to the hotel, his hand clutching mine tightly the entire drive.

When we got to my room, I didn't know what to expect. It wasn't him crushing me into a hug so fierce that it was hard to breathe. It wasn't Chad pulling me toward the bed and wrapping his large, warm body around me. He was quiet, but his hold never wavered. We both were in and out of sleep last night, restless from what we knew was coming.

No matter how many times I tried, I couldn't put into words what I was feeling. I knew that I needed to be his pillar of support, which was a feat not letting my fear show.

We have days before he ships out. *Days.* My visit here will be cut short. Tears well in my eyes from the knowledge that he's going overseas. I'm so glad I accepted his invitation to come and visit.

I don't want him to go.

My tears begin rolling down my cheeks. I try to choke them back, but it's no use.

"I'm here." Chad wraps his arms even tighter around my waist and buries his face in my neck. "I'm right here." My body shakes with silent sobs. I know I should be strong for him, but the fear of losing him is choking me. I can feel it in my throat every time I swallow.

"I'm sorry." The sorrow in my voice is like a knife twisting in my soul.

"Baby, no," he says, kissing my shoulder. "I know this is hard for you."

"You're the one leaving. You're the one putting your life on the line. I'm supposed to be strong for you. I'm supposed to be your support system."

"You are here for me. I'm holding you. There is nothing in this world I'd rather be doing on my last days here than this."

"I hate your job. I know that's selfish of me, but I do, Chad. I hate it. I know what you do is selfless and admirable, but it's taking you even farther away from me. I hate that so much." Tears run freely down my cheeks.

He doesn't comment, and I didn't expect him to. Chad, just like my brother, is honorable. He loves his country, and he loves what he does. He may hate that this job is taking him away from me, but it's his duty, one he's honored and proud to be a part of. I love him even more for it.

Rolling over, I place my hand on his cheek. "Promise me you'll be safe." My words are whispered, but the plea and the desperation are clear.

"I promise."

"Promise me you'll come home to me."

Something flashes in his eyes, but it's gone before I can name it. "I promise you I'll do everything in my power to come home to you." He pulls me in and presses his lips to my forehead.

He didn't promise me he was coming home, but we both pretend like I don't notice. I know it's not fair to ask that of him, but my heart wants to hear him tell me everything is going to be okay.

"What do you want to do today?" he asks.

"I don't care as long as I'm with you."

"I don't go back to work, outside of a few meetings, before we leave. I want to spend every second that I'm not there with you."

I nod, unable to speak because I'm afraid nothing will come out of my mouth but the sob I keep trying to choke back.

"How about we get ready and go grab some breakfast? We can do some sightseeing."

I nod my agreement.

"You want to shower first?"

"No. You go ahead." He kisses the corner of my mouth before sliding out of bed and heading toward the shower. As soon as the door closes and the water turns on, the sob I was trying to contain breaks free. I allow myself a few minutes to let it all out before climbing out of bed, and gathering my clothes. I have to hold it in. I can be sad, but I can't let him see how much this hurts.

I can't let myself think about the what-ifs.

I can't let myself think about losing him.

"I'm so full." I push my plate away from me. We're sitting in a small diner on the edge of town and I feel as though I just ate my weight in pancakes and bacon.

"You barely touched it." Chad digs his fork into my leftover pancakes and takes a huge bite.

"Did you see the size of that stack? It's over halfway gone," I argue.

"Lightweight," he teases, taking another bite, before placing his fork and napkin on his now empty plate.

"We all can't be human garbage disposals." I stick my tongue out at him, and he laughs.

He lifts his shirt. "I burn a lot of calories to keep this." He runs his hands over his washboard abs.

"Can you please put your shirt down? People are trying to eat." I pretend like he's offending people, when really all he's doing is making my mouth water.

"You jealous, baby?" he asks. His eyes sparkle with mischief, and I make sure to lock that look away, to memorize it so I have something to hold on to while he's gone.

"No." Kind of, but I'd never tell him that.

"Uh-huh." He chuckles. "Let me pay the bill, and we can go."

"I can—" I start to reach for my purse, but the look he gives me changes my mind. "So bossy." I playfully roll my eyes.

"You know you don't pay when you're with me." He grabs the ticket and makes his way to the counter.

I pull my phone out of my purse to have something to do while I wait. When I pull up my email app, I freeze when I see an email with the subject line *Request for interview*. I tap on the screen and quickly read. I have to read it three times before I do a little shimmy in my seat, because this is what I've been waiting for.

"What's the dance for?" Chad asks.

"This." I thrust my phone at him.

His eyes scan the screen. "Kindergarten." He smiles as he continues to read. "Wait." He pulls his eyes from the phone to stare at me. "You applied here?"

"What?"

"Faith, this job is in California. It's actually in this town."

"What?" I say again, my enthusiasm deflated.

"Come on." Chad keeps my phone in one hand and offers me the other. I place my hand in his and he helps me stand from the booth. His fingers twine through mine as he leads me outside to the rental. We're both quiet as he leads me to the passenger side and opens the door for me. Once I'm in, he closes the door and rushes around the car before sliding behind the wheel. He doesn't start the car, instead, turns in his seat to face me. "Talk to me."

"I'm just bummed. This is what I've been hoping for, and it's here. In California."

"How did you find the job?"

I shrug. "Social media. I guess I didn't realize my phone adjusted my location when I was looking for jobs online. I was so excited I'd found a kindergarten position, I didn't even look at where it was."

He nods. "So, what are you going to do?" He reaches over and laces his fingers with mine.

"What do you mean?" His hand in mine is soothing.

"Are you going to take the interview?"

"Why would I? I live in Ohio, Chad. Are you losing your mind in your old age?" I tease. I'm trying like hell not to show my disappointment. The past two days have been extreme highs and extreme lows. I'll have time to stress over my job after I send him off. He doesn't need me piling my worries on him right now.

"I'm being serious. Take the interview. What's the worst that can happen?"

"Um, that I'll get the job when I don't live here." That would be my luck. I'd be offered the position on the spot and have to turn it down. Talk about depressing.

"Consider it experience. Besides, I'm here."

Is he saying I should stay here? In California? "But you're leaving."

"I'll only be gone for four to six months."

"That's a long time."

He shrugs. "It's not even a year. I think you should do it."

My heart starts to race at the possibility of getting my dream job and living close to Chad when he comes home. He's going to come home. "I'm just setting myself up for disappointment. What happens if they offer me the job?"

"That depends. Do you like the school? Do you like the interview team? Do you like the location? Do you feel safe there? Do you want to live close to me?" He winks. "There are a lot of questions that would need answers."

"But I don't live here." I sound like a broken record, but that's all I can manage as I struggle to process what he's suggesting.

"Then move here."

"What?" My heart is no longer racing. It's soaring. Does he want us to be together? Is that what he's telling me? Are we finally going to be in the right place at the right time? No. He's leaving. I'm letting my heart get confused. He just wants me to be happy, and he knows this is my dream. What he doesn't know is that he's also my dream. I'd give up my dream of being a kindergarten teacher if the choice was Chad or my job.

"Move here. I'm here."

"You won't be," I blurt out the obvious.

Sadness fills his eyes, and his shoulders slump. "I know, but you have Hannah here, and you're the most down-to-earth person I've ever met. I have no doubt you'll meet new people."

"You want me to move to California? From Ohio?" I add, because I feel like it's worth repeating.

"I know where you currently live, Faith. You were willing to look outside of the area at home if you could get kindergarten. This is outside of your area."

"This is not even in the same state."

He shrugs. "Chase your dreams, baby."

"I can't just pack up and move."

"Why?" There's challenge in his eyes.

"I just… can't."

"Faith Gregory, you can." He leans over the console, and I find myself gravitating toward him. "You can do anything you want. This is your dream job. Chase it. You don't have to make a decision. Just accept the interview. Consider it good experience and interview training."

"I don't want to waste their time."

"You won't be. You could leave there with your dream job."

"In California."

"Yes."

"This is crazy."

"You don't have a lease or a mortgage to worry about. There is nothing holding you back."

"I'd need a place to live. I can't stay in the hotel forever." He stares deep into my eyes, as if he's begging me to understand the unspoken words that flow between us. I wish I could hear what he's thinking.

"I'll help you."

"You're leaving."

He nods stiffly. "Hannah. She's going to be here on her own too. I'm sure she wouldn't mind you staying with her until we get back, or until you find your own place." He stops and opens his mouth as if he's going to say something else, but quickly closes it.

"I can't just call Hannah, someone I've met twice, and say hey, I'm moving across the country, so can I stay with you? Do you hear how crazy that sounds?"

"Trust me." His eyes bore into mine. "Just go on the interview. Treat this as if it were a job back in Cooper. Go, then come home to me, and we can talk about it."

"I'm afraid to go. This is what I've always wanted, Chad. To have it dangling in front of me, and lose it—" I shake my head. If I do this, and I get the job, it will hurt even more to have to turn it down. I can't just uproot my life and move to California. My family is in Ohio. This is crazy and harmful to my heart, but there is still a huge part of me that wants to go to the interview just to see if they would pick me.

He lifts our entwined hands to his lips and kisses my knuckles. "I want you to have your dream, Faith. Please, just trust me. Go on this interview. I have a good feeling about this."

"I can't move here and you be gone. I'm already going to miss you too much." Tears well in my eyes.

"I'll be back before you know it."

As crazy as it sounds, moving here would make me feel closer to him even when he's deployed. It's risky, but there is something in my gut telling me that it's a risk worth taking. "Okay."

"Okay?"

I nod. "I'll reply and accept the interview. I hate that it's going to take some of the time we have together."

"Take the afternoon spot. I have a meeting in the afternoon. We'll both be busy at the same time. I'm glad you're going to go. We can talk about the rest when you get home."

"The rest of what?"

"The future."

His reply is vague, but I don't comment on it. My head is too jumbled with the possibility of moving here, of uprooting my life when the one person I know is about to leave the country for four to six months. My heart is too busy trying to beat out of my chest at the thought of Chad and I finally being more. Is that why he's pushing for this? I'm too afraid to ask him.

I'll go to that interview, and then, when we're both back in the room, we can talk about it, just like he said. Maybe by then, I'll have enough courage to ask him.

I'm pacing the hotel room, waiting for Chad to get here. I'm surprised there's not a path worn in the carpet yet. I've only been here for twenty minutes, but my pacing has been nonstop.

The interview was… incredible. So much so that I was offered the job on the spot. I've never been this happy and sad at the same time before. It's my dream job. The people I met today were great. The classroom was perfect. It's everything, but I don't live here. Yes, I was willing to drive a little farther, but this is across the country.

Can I do that?

Can I pack up and live in a state where the only person I know is leaving for four to six months? I'd be starting over, and all on my own. That's scary as hell, and I'm conflicted. I want to do it. I wanted to shout yes when they offered me the job, but I'm also scared to take the leap.

The door opens, and I freeze. Chad walks into the room and smiles when he sees me. "How did it go?"

I swallow hard, trying to calm myself down. "Incredible."

"Yeah?" His eyes light up.

"I loved the school. The room that would be my classroom was perfect and had so much potential, and the principal and superintendent were both wonderful and easy to talk to. I felt as though we were old friends catching up. It didn't feel like an interview at all."

"Come here." He stalks toward me and wraps his arms around me. "I'm so happy for you." He holds me close, and I return his embrace with everything I have.

"It's my dream job."

"Hell yes," he says, releasing me, and taking a step back.

"It sucks I have to turn it down." My shoulders drop as my excitement deflates.

"What? Why would you turn it down? Faith, this is what you've been waiting for. You've been on a ton of interviews, and not once have I heard you this excited."

"I just—you're leaving, Chad. I'd be here all alone. I don't have a place to live. The only person I know is Hannah, and we just met. It's crazy. I can't uproot my life just because I selfishly want this job."

"You can. Be selfish, Faith. Put yourself first. This is your dream job. Baby, you haven't stopped smiling since I walked through the door." He steps closer and cradles my face in the palm of his hands. "I'm coming home to you. Four to six months, and then it's you and me."

My eyes well with tears. "You and me?"

"Yes."

"What does that mean?" I whisper the words, afraid of his reply. The way he's looking at me makes me think it's more, but it's too risky to let my heart take the lead. I need to use my head, and it's better if we clear the air, even if the question has panic building in my chest.

"Do you trust me?"

"Yes." It's the truth. I trust this man with my life.

"I'll take care of everything. Just take the job, Faith."

"How are you going to take care of everything? You won't be here!" I yell and instantly regret it. "You won't be here," I say again, this time with no anger, just pain and sorrow because he's standing right in front of me and I already miss him. "You're leaving me."

"Listen to me." He tilts my head so that we're eye to eye. "I don't give a damn where I am in this world. I'm always with you. Do you hear me? Always. I don't care about the miles between us. I'm still right here." He takes my hand and places it over his heart. "You're right here with me. Always."

I can't stop the tears. "I can't do this on my own."

"Then let me help you."

"How? How can you help me when you're leaving? I know it's your job, and I'm not trying to be a brat, but how? I don't understand how this is going to work."

He presses my hand harder against his chest, and I can feel his heart racing beneath my palm. He studies me for several heartbeats before dropping to one knee. "Marry me."

Time freezes, and everything around me blurs. Everything except for this incredible man on one knee asking me to be his.

Chapter 11

Chad

FAITH LOOKS AT ME LIKE I'VE GROWN A SECOND HEAD.

"What?" she whisper-yells, her eyes as wide as the plates we ate off of last night.

I can't help but smile. "Marry me. I know I don't have a ring, but I'll get you one. Me too."

She shakes her head as a bubble of nervous laughter spills from her lips. There's also a slight tremble to her hand as I take it in my own. "You're nuts."

"Maybe, but it's one of my most endearing qualities," I tease, flashing a charismatic grin her way. "In all seriousness, I'll do everything in my power to protect you, Faith. Everything. This is the perfect solution. You can take your dream job, and I'll be able to apply for married housing. Since I'm being sent away, I'm sure they'll grant it immediately. I know you'll be safe here. You'll have Hannah, and I'm certain making more friends in no time."

My heart is trying to beat out of my chest, because all I want to do is tell her how much I love her, but that's not what we agreed to. *Friends.* Okay, friends who get a little intimate from time to time, but our relationship is based on a solid foundation of friendship. I will do everything in my power to make her happy, and that includes marrying her.

It's definitely not a hardship.

"I know it sounds crazy, but it feels right," I confess, a small smile curling my lips. "We can get married by the chaplain on base tomorrow, and I'll make sure all of the paperwork is taken care of. You'll be added to my insurance, and I know you don't want to hear this, but you'll receive death benefits if something happens to me."

She whimpers, her eyes filling with tears.

"It's the best way I can both protect and honor you, Faith. Don't be scared, sweetheart. Marry me."

There's a mixture of hope and fear swirling in the depths of her eyes. "This is crazy," she whispers, the faintest grin on her lush lips, and I know I have her.

"Maybe, but I think it's right. It feels that way here," I tell her, tapping my chest where my heart pounds like a drum.

Faith exhales and closes her eyes. She gives her head a slight shake, and when she looks down at me again, she says, "Marry you for four to six months?"

I know what she's thinking. She knows I want to protect her while I'm deployed, in case something happens to me. What she doesn't realize is I want it all. With her. I nod and reply, "For starters."

The truth is there's no way in hell I'll be able to ever let her go.

She'll always be mine and own my soul.

"My parents are going to kill me," she blurts with a laugh.

"Does that mean…?"

Grinning widely, she offers me the most breathtaking smile I've ever seen. It reaches into my chest and calms every wild and unsettled piece of me. She's the missing puzzle piece I didn't even know I was searching for. "Yes."

A loud whoop flies from my mouth, and I jump up, taking her in my arms. The moment she's settled against my chest, I slide my hands into her hair and gaze down at her. "You're really going to marry me?"

She giggles and nods. "I am. I don't know if we're doing the right thing or not, but I can't let you go overseas worrying about me."

I snort. "I'll always worry about you, sweetheart. Always. But having my ring on your finger will go a long way at soothing some of that fear I have over being away from you."

She swallows hard. "I understand, and all I want to do is keep you from worrying more. The last thing I'd want is you to be distracted and get yourself blown up or something."

"You're the best kind of distraction," I state, speaking the truth even when she thinks I'm joking.

She wraps her arms around my waist and leans against my chest. I'm certain she can hear the thundering in my chest. "I can't believe we're getting married," she murmurs softly before turning to look up at me. "And I'm going to accept that job," she adds with a giggle.

"Hell yes, you are. You're going to be the most kick-ass kindergarten teacher this school has ever seen. I have complete faith in you, no pun intended."

She shakes her head as if she's still trying to process everything that's happened in just a short amount of time. "I feel like we have so much to do."

I step back and slide my hands along the column of her neck, up her jaw, and into her hair. "We do, but first, I want to kiss my fiancée."

Nervously nibbling on the corner of her lip, she whispers, "Your fiancée would like that."

Keeping my eyes open as long as I can, I finally close them and just revel in the first brush of our lips together. The kiss starts slow, as if we both want to savor the magnitude of this moment. And it's pretty fucking big. I asked her to marry me, and she accepted. As far as kisses go, it doesn't get much bigger than this.

I coax her lips apart with my tongue and slide mine inside against hers. Her hands fist my T-shirt at my sides as she leans forward and presses her chest to my own. I can feel her nipples through the layers of material, and my cock starts paying closer attention.

As much as I want to just keep kissing her for hours on end, I reluctantly pull back, slipping a little distance between us so I can get my raging libido under control. The truth is we have a lot to do and very little time to do it.

Faith opens her eyes and gives me a shy little grin. Her lips are swollen, her hair a bit tussled from my hands, and all I want to do is reach for her and continue that kiss. "Well, my to-do list between now and Wednesday morning just got a bit longer."

"No shit," I reply with a snort. "How about this? I need to go to the base and apply for married housing and talk to the chaplain. You need to accept that job offer immediately."

"I need to do more than that if we're getting married tomorrow," she states.

I prepare to head for the door, when something causes me to pause. "Your parents."

She gives me a sad smile. "Look, as much as I'd love them to be here, I don't think it's possible. It would cost so much for an immediate flight out here, and it just seems like such a hassle. I know I've only had a few minutes to think about this, but what if we just did it and asked for forgiveness later?" She bites down on her bottom lip nervously, and I almost lose my ability to keep my groan from flying from my mouth.

"I want whatever you want."

"I'd want your parents to be here too. And Ford and Shayne. It just seems like the best step here would be to elope and tell them afterward."

I don't miss the sadness flooding her eyes as she says those words. "How about this?" I start, taking a step toward her and reaching for her hand. "What if we FaceTime with them? We can have Erik and Hannah serve as our witnesses, and they can hold the phone. Maybe even two phones. Whatever we have to do."

My words seem to flush any unease right out of those green eyes. "That might work," she says eagerly, yet it doesn't completely erase the hurt I see at knowing her family won't be in attendance at our wedding.

"Good. I'll be back shortly. We can call our families tonight, if you want. In the meantime, if you think of anything else, text me."

"Okay." She nods as I turn to head for the door once more. "Wait! What are we supposed to wear? I didn't exactly pack a wedding dress in my luggage."

"You'll be beautiful in anything you wear," I tell her honestly.

She swallows thickly and blushes. "Uhh, okay. What are you going to wear?"

A smile tugs on my lips. "My full dress uniform."

Her eyes widen just a bit. "I can't wear jean shorts if you're in your dress uniform," she mutters.

"You can wear whatever you want, darlin.'"

"There's that secondhand place on the main drag in town. Maybe I can find something there," she says, almost absently to herself.

"I'm serious, Faith," I tell her, returning to where she stands and placing my hands on her upper arms. "Wear whatever you want."

She nods once, and my lips find their way to hers once more. This kiss is chaste, though, and not nearly long enough. But we have a lot to do this afternoon and the sooner I get back to the base, the sooner I set everything else into motion.

"I'll be back."

"All right. See you soon," she replies just before I shut the door to her hotel room.

I can't believe this is happening. I'm going to marry Faith. Tomorrow. And not entirely for a sense of duty.

I *want* to marry her, make her mine, and even though she insinuated it would be for four to six months, I have no intention of ending it. Once I have my ring on her finger, I will do whatever it takes to ensure it stays there for the rest of our lives.

What once was friendship has grown into something more.

Something great.

This is only the beginning.

I'm smiling as I leave the chaplain's office with the paperwork we need to complete for tomorrow's ceremony. He ensured me he'd be ready at noon but requested we arrive by eleven thirty to finalize the paperwork with the administrative assistant, Lois. Knowing that I'll be marrying her in less than twenty-four hours has added an extra spring to my step.

My next stop is the administrative office where I will take care of adding Faith as my wife and apply for married housing. I walk to the building and give my name and reason for being there to the security team inside the door. They direct me to the correct office, which is just a short walk down the main corridor and to the right.

"Good afternoon," I greet as I enter the office.

"Hello. How may I help you?"

I go through my reason for being here and earn a wide smile from the woman at the desk. "Wow, congratulations. There are several forms you'll need to fill out, and some that cannot be submitted until after the wedding ceremony tomorrow," she informs me, pulling different folders out of a filing cabinet and placing them on the desk.

"Can I turn them all in tomorrow?" I ask, wanting to get back to Faith as quickly as I can.

"Sure can. Just bring these all back, along with your pretty new wife. I'll get the ball rolling for your application for married housing. In light of your deployment on Wednesday, we can expedite the process and get you into a unit as soon as possible. It might not be before you leave, though."

"That's fine. I'll make sure she has help moving," I tell the woman, making a mental note for when I leave. I'm certain Hannah will be able to assist her, but it would be helpful to have extra aid.

Especially with me out of the country.

"Thank you, ma'am," I reply, gathering the newest stack of papers and exiting the office.

"You're welcome."

When I reach outside, I pull out my phone and fire off a text message.

> **Me:** Two more stops and then I'll be back to the hotel.
>
> **Faith:** Hannah is picking me up in ten minutes. We're going shopping.

A smile spreads across my face at the thought of Faith purchasing something to wear to our wedding.

> **Me:** No rush. Have fun. I'll see you soon.
>
> **Faith:** Be safe.
>
> **Me:** You too.

I decide to add purchasing a car to the list, but know that might not get done before I leave. There's a used lot in town which caters to members of the military living on this base and their families. Faith is going to need something reliable to get around town, and everyone recommends buying from Lon's Used Cars.

I head over to the barracks next to retrieve my dress uniform. Everything else, I'll pack up into two bags—the stuff I'm taking with me and what I'm leaving behind. Fortunately, the barracks is empty when I arrive, so I don't have to answer a dozen questions about why I'm packing up today and not closer to Wednesday's departure. I leave what I'll be taking with me on my bed and grab the small duffle bag with the items Faith will have to transfer to our new place. There isn't much in it, but I know I can only take the basics with me overseas.

Finally, I head out of the barracks. The sun is beating down on my head, but I ignore the way sweat instantly starts to form on my forehead and upper lip. I throw my bag and hang my dress uniform in the rental car and climb behind the wheel. The moment the car is fired up, I pull out my cell phone. Before I make my final stop, there's one conversation I need to have.

Ford answers on the second ring.

"What the hell are you doing calling in the middle of the day? Shouldn't you be working or with my sister?" he asks. A smile instantly spreads across my mouth at the sound of his voice.

"Had a few errands to run."

There's a pause before he asks, "Everything all right? Faith?"

Just the mention of her name has me grinning. "She's fine. Perfect, actually." Clearing my throat, I decide to rip off the Band-Aid. "I'm being sent overseas."

"Shit. When?"

"Wednesday. 0600."

"Fuck, man, I'm sorry."

"Thanks, but that's not entirely the reason I called you."

"Okay," he replies, drawing out that single word.

"I need you to try to rally the troops and get them here by noon tomorrow." I'm met with silence once more. "Are you there?"

"Yeah," he replies, clearing his throat. "It sounded like you want me in California in less than twenty-four hours."

"I do. You, Shayne, your parents, and my parents. Cassie, too, if she's able to get away. I know it's a tall ask," I start, letting him cut me off.

"You're asking me to get all these people on a plane to California first thing tomorrow morning?"

My heart is pounding in my chest. "Yes. That's exactly what I'm asking."

He blows out a deep breath. "That's... wow. I'll see what I can do. You know I'll have everyone there if I can. Mom is out of school still for the summer, so I'm sure she and Dad can make it. I'll email my boss now to request emergency time off, and I'll see if Shayne can rearrange her clients. I'm not sure about your parents and sister, but I'll try."

Exhaling in relief, I reply, "That's all I ask. Thanks, man. I owe you one."

"No, you don't," he states with conviction. Then he adds, "Can you tell me what this is about? It feels like there's something more than just wanting us all there to see you off."

I want to tell him everything, but I also don't want to risk Faith finding out what I've done. It's one of the few things I can do for her before I leave. I can give her a wedding with our families, as well as their support when I ship out Wednesday. "I'll explain when you get here," is all I say.

I can tell it's not what he wants to hear, but he eventually replies, "Fine. I have vacation time built up, and as long as Shayne can move clients to another day, we'll be there. I'm sure Mom and Dad will be too."

"My parents will agree. Cassie too."

At least I hope so.

She's finishing college, earning her teaching degree in art. Since it's the tail end of summer break, I hope she can find a few days to get away and join us.

"Text me a number and I'll get hotel rooms at the place Faith is staying," I tell him, checking the time on the dash.

"Give me an hour or so."

"Take the time you need."

"Chad," Ford says, seriousness and uncertainty in his voice. "You're sure everything's all right?"

I can't help but smile. "Everything's exactly as it's supposed to be."

With a sigh, he says, "Fine. See you tomorrow, man."

"Can't wait."

Hanging up, I set my phone down in the cupholder and slowly back out of the parking space. I have one more stop to make, and I hope Faith and Hannah don't catch me. The shop I'm visiting is about a block away from the secondhand clothing store they're going to, but I think I can slip in without being seen.

I park around the corner and keep my head down as I walk to the pawn shop. The bell chimes as I open the door and slip inside.

"Good afternoon."

"Hi," I reply to the older gentleman behind the counter.

"Are you looking for something specific?"

"Yes, sir. I'm looking for an engagement and wedding ring set."

He smiles widely. "I have a decent selection for you to choose from," he tells me, waving toward the glass case near the register.

The moment I start to scan the display, my eyes settle on a pair in the back row. "That one," I state, pointing to my choice.

Again, he grins, reaching into the locked case. "Excellent choice, young man. She's going to love it."

He places them in my palm and gives me a minute to inspect the two rings. My heart is beating wildly in my chest as I gaze down at the simple pear-shaped diamond set on a rose gold band with small diamonds set within both rings.

It's perfect.

It's her.

It's *the* ring.

And I'm going to love seeing it on her finger.

"I'll take it."

Chapter 12

Faith

I'M GETTING MARRIED.

Tomorrow.

I have a dress. It's a white spaghetti-strap summer dress with lace around the waist. It's simple and elegant and could easily pass for a wedding dress. It's perfect, and as soon as I laid eyes on it, I wanted it. I was sure it wouldn't be my size, but as luck would have it, it was. I immediately tried it on, and was sold. First dress, first store. I was one and done.

Hannah and I then went to the local florist and were able to order a bouquet that the owner made while we waited. Once we told her I was getting married before my fiancé was shipped off, she insisted.

My fiancé.

Somehow, overnight everything in my life seemed to fall into place. I have the job of my dreams, and the man, the one I've been in love with since the moment we met, dropped to one knee to ask me to marry him. Sure, it's temporary, but maybe, if I'm lucky, we can explore this connection we share, and when he comes home, we can skip the divorce and ride off into the happily-ever-after sunset.

I'll make the house we're assigned a home for him. For us. Chad and I have been dancing around this connection for far too long. It's time to do something about it, and the moment he dropped to one knee, I knew my answer. I was going to say yes to him, and then fight like hell to make this marriage permanent.

My hands are shaking as I reach for the hotel room door. Chad is already back. I saw the rental car in the parking lot. My dress is in a bag, so I don't have to worry about him seeing it. Not that this is a traditional wedding, anyway. Our families are not even going to be here. I hate that they're going to miss this. I only plan to be married once. Maybe, once he's home, we can renew our vows or something?

One step at a time.

Pushing open the door, I step into the room that's been my home away from home, during my time here. "Hey." I smile when I see Chad sitting at the small two-person dining table.

"There's my fiancée. Did you find a dress?" He stands and greets me with a kiss.

"I did." I hold up the garment bag. "And flowers." I hold up the bouquet in my other hand.

"Perfect."

"What are you doing?" I ask as he sits back down at the table.

"Filling out paperwork for the wedding and married housing. They're going to expedite it, but they can't until after the marriage license is signed. We'll have to stop and drop all of this stuff off tomorrow." He signs a few more papers before handing me the pen. "Your turn. Make sure you sign Faith Anthony."

I freeze, my eyes locked on his. "Okay." I slowly nod.

"Date it for tomorrow."

My hand shakes just a little as I sign my name, my new name, next to where the forms require a spouse's signature. We're really doing this. I'm going to be Mrs. Chad Anthony.

Once I'm finished, I hand him the pen. "We're all set. I have my dress blues; they're hanging in the closet. Everything is scheduled for tomorrow. Hannah and Erik will be there as well."

"Is there anything I need to do?"

"Yes, actually. I bought a car today. We need to go pick it up and then take the rental back so you don't have to deal with it on your own."

"You bought a car?"

"I did. You need a permanent means of transportation while I'm gone, and a long-term rental would have been expensive."

"What did you buy?" I don't know how I manage to speak the words with the lump in my throat. He's going out of his way to make sure I have what I'll need while he's deployed. My heart swells to the point it feels too large for my chest.

"A Toyota Camry. It's a couple of years old, but only has twenty thousand miles."

"Wow."

He steps up next to me and wraps me in his arms. "I need to make sure my wife is taken care of."

"You do. You have, I just—I didn't expect you to buy a car."

"A car, a new house, and this." He pulls back and drops to his knee for the second time today.

I watch closely as he reaches into his pocket and pulls out a small ring box. Opening it, he plucks something out, and rests the box on the floor next to him. Taking my hand, he smiles up at me. "I didn't have this earlier, but that's okay. I have it now. Faith Gregory, will you do me the incredible honor of becoming my wife? Will you marry me?"

My heart pounds in my chest, and tears pool in my eyes. It's the same exact overwhelming emotions coursing through my veins the second time around. This time with a gorgeous diamond ring being offered to me.

"Yes." Tears roll down my cheeks and my hand shakes as he slips the diamond onto my finger.

Chad stands, pulls me into his arms, and kisses me. The kiss steals the breath from my lungs. When he finally pulls away, he rests his forehead against mine. "My wife," he murmurs.

"My husband."

His grip on my hips tightens at the name, and that gives me hope. So much hope and light inside my heart that this isn't just temporary. That this could be—no, that this will be, our happily ever after.

"Nervous?" Chad asks. His fingers are laced with mine as we reach the chapel on base.

"No. Are you?"

He scoffs. "I'm marrying my girl today. What's there to be nervous about?"

His words have my heart melting inside my chest. Sometimes, the things he says, it makes me think this is more than just an arrangement while he's deployed. Either way, I'm pushing that out of my mind, and today, I'm going to pretend. I'm going to give the day my full attention, because I hope with everything inside me, this is my one and only wedding. It's a day I never want to forget.

Pushing open the doors to the chapel, we take a few steps and then I freeze. Standing before us are our families. My parents, my brother with Shayne, Chad's parents and his younger sister, they're all here.

Chad squeezes my hand. Then again, maybe I'm the one doing the squeezing.

"Chad?" I ask, fighting back tears. I want to look at him, but I can't seem to take my eyes off the group of people who are the most special to us standing in front of me.

Chad leans in, placing his lips next to my ear. His words are soft and only for me. "Surprise, wife. We can't get married without our families."

I find the strength to turn to face him as tears well in my eyes. "You did this for me?"

Lifting his hand, he wipes at my tears with his thumb. "Nothing I wouldn't do for you, Faith."

It takes everything I am to not blurt out how much I love this man. Thankfully, my brother steps forward and stops me.

"What's going on?" Ford asks. He watches me closely with suspicion in his gaze.

"You don't know?" I ask my brother.

"All I know is that Chad called and said I needed to get everyone here by noon today."

Chad drops my hand and slides his arm around my waist. "Thank you all for coming. I know it was short notice, but we needed our families here for this."

"Here for what?" my dad asks. He glances from me to Chad, wearing the same suspicious gaze as my brother.

"Chad and I are getting married today." I watch as my father processes that information. He swallows hard and nods. My eyes move to Mom and there are tears in her eyes.

"Married?" Ford asks.

"I asked Faith to marry me and she said yes. I'm being shipped out tomorrow, and we didn't want to wait. She'll be moving into married housing later this week, and I hope that some of you can stay to help her."

"Son, you know we will," Chad's dad speaks up.

"Thank you for being here. All of you," Chad tells them. He releases his hold on me and steps in front of my dad. "I'm sorry I didn't get to talk to you first, but this was so last minute, there wasn't time to do things in order. Sir, I love your daughter. She's my best friend. I want to marry her. I'd love your blessing, but please understand we don't need it."

"Chad," I scold as I try to process what he's just said. I know it's to ease my parents' minds, but my heart didn't seem to get that memo. He sounds sincere, and oh how I wish that's what this wedding's about.

He turns to me and smiles. "We're doing this, Faith. You and me." He holds his hand out for me, and I take it.

"This is what you want?" my father asks.

"Yeah, Chad and I have talked about this. This is what we want." It's not me confessing my undying love, but it's enough for my father if the softening of his eyes is any indication.

"I'm so excited!" Shayne rushes forward and pulls me into a hug. Ford does the same to Chad before they switch.

"You chose well, big brother," Cassie says, drawing me into a hug first.

"Hey!" Chad protests.

"Get used to it, brother. You're giving me the sister I've always wanted." Cassie winks before releasing me from her grip and giving her brother the same affection.

Our parents take their turn, and then it's time. Erik and Hannah are here, and although we asked them to be our witnesses, it's Ford and Shayne who stand up with us. The wedding hasn't even started, and it's perfect. I know this is a day I will never forget.

Standing in front of the chaplain, the ceremony begins. We told him short and sweet, and that's what we get. Tears burn my eyes, but my smile is so wide, I feel as though my face might crack. The conflicting emotions battle with one another. Happy tears, happy smiles, and the man I've wanted to be mine vowing to love me in sickness and in health.

"I do," I say when it's my turn.

Chad smiles. It's soft, and if I didn't know better, full of love.

"I do," he repeats.

"By the power vested in me, I now pronounce you husband and wife. You may kiss the bride."

"The best part," Chad says, not bothering to lower his voice, as our family and friends laugh. His hands cradle my cheeks as he stares into my eyes. "My wife." His voice is gruff with emotion.

My hands rise to cover his. "My husband." My voice cracks.

He leans in close, and I lick my lips. His eyes follow the action as his hot breath fans across my face. His eyes shutter closed, and I do the same at the feel of his lips pressing to mine. It's chaste at first, but I moan, because how can I not? I'm kissing my husband.

My. Husband.

Chad groans, his tongue tracing my lips, and suddenly it doesn't matter who's watching. We allow ourselves to get lost in one another. That is until my brother speaks up.

"Come on, man," Ford groans. "That's my little sister."

Chad laughs and pulls out of the kiss that I'll remember for a lifetime, resting his forehead against mine. His chest rises and falls with silent laughter. "My wife," he says loudly, knowing Ford and everyone else will hear him. Then, "I'll never get tired of saying that," is whispered in a low tone. Those words just for me.

Clapping and cheers greet us, and the moment is broken.

Chad stands back to his full height and laces our fingers. He lifts my left hand to his lips and places a kiss over my engagement ring and wedding band. I reach for his left hand and rub my thumb over the band that now sits on his finger. Our eyes lock, and my heart stutters. I open my mouth to tell him that I love him, but before the words can pass my lips, my brother is there, pulling me away from my husband. He lifts me off my feet and spins us in a circle.

"My little sister just made my best friend my brother. Best day ever!"

"Hey!" Shayne scolds him playfully.

"Until we get married, baby." Ford kisses the protest from her lips.

"Thank you all for being here. My wife and I have some paperwork to turn in since I'm leaving in the morning. We have a reserved dining room at the hotel restaurant where we're all staying for the Anthony wedding. We'll meet you there."

We take the time to hug everyone before getting into our new-to-us Camry and driving to the other side of base to turn in our marriage license and the rest of our paperwork. I pinch my thigh to see if I can feel the pain. The pain is there, which means this is real. I'm married.

Chad Anthony is my husband.

Chad pulls into the hotel's parking lot and turns off the engine. Neither one of us makes a move to leave the confines of the car. I can't stop thinking about how we have mere hours left before he has to leave, and it will be at least four months, possibly longer, before I get to feel his strong arms wrap around me.

The process of the paperwork was easy, and then we stopped at the bank to add me to all of Chad's accounts. I fought him on it, but the look he gave me told me what he wouldn't say. There is always a chance something could go wrong and he might not come home. He wanted me to have full access to his life, including his money.

I didn't want to think about it, but I signed my name where necessary and shoved my shiny new Faith Anthony debit card into my purse for safekeeping.

"You okay, wife?"

I turn to glance at him. A swarm of butterflies are flapping their wings in my belly. I'm a wife. Not just a wife, but his. "I'm going to miss you." My voice breaks, and tears start to form in my eyes.

"I'll miss you too. I hate that you're finally mine, and I have to leave you."

"What do I do? While you're gone?"

"You start your new job. You'll be so busy setting up your classroom and settling in that you won't have time to miss me."

"Don't say that. You know that's not true."

"I know, but I want you to enjoy this. It's what you've always wanted.

Your dream of becoming a kindergarten teacher is here. I want to hear about it. Every day, emails, letters, and I'll call when I can."

"Do you know how often that will be?"

"No, but I'm hoping pretty often." He rests his hand against my cheek. "I wish I were going to be here to see you live your dream."

"You won't miss it. I'll make sure you hear about every minute. You're going to get tired of my letters, emails, and text messages."

"Never, wife. Never will I get tired of anything that involves you."

I lean into his touch, his words making my heart feel like a gooey mess of love. "How will I get your things to move them to the house?"

"I'm already packed. Everything that I'm not taking with me is in the hotel room."

"That's all you have?"

He shrugs. "I'm a simple man. Living in the barracks doesn't offer a lot of space. Not like a house I'll be sharing with my wife."

"You keep saying that. Calling me your wife."

"Do you want me to stop?"

"No."

"Good. Wife." He grins. "I have a lot of money saved up. They give us everything we need here, so use the account for the car and rent, and whatever else we need to make our house a home."

"Don't you want to pick out what you're going to be living with once you get home?"

"Come on, baby, you know what they say, happy wife, happy life." He smiles.

"Stop." I shake my head. My smile rivals his. So much has happened in a short amount of time, and I already know I'll never grow tired of hearing him refer to me as his wife.

"I'm being serious. I want to return to a home. Not just a house. I want you to be there, and I want it to be everything you dreamed it would be."

"What about what you want?"

"I got the girl, Faith. There isn't a single thing I can think of that I want more."

My heart swells, but I ignore it. I can't let myself fall into the belief that this is anything more than convenience. "But once you're home—" I start, but can't seem to find the words to bring up the fact that we're doing this just for while he's deployed. I don't want to remind myself or him that this isn't real.

"I'll be coming back to the home my wife built for us. Now, we have family who's waiting to celebrate with us. I love them all, but I really want this meal to be over with so I can spend some time with my wife, just you and me, before I have to leave in the morning." He leans over the console and softly presses his lips to mine. "You ready?"

I suck in a deep breath and square my shoulders. I'm not ready, but I have to be. I have to be strong for him. That's my job as a military wife, right? I need to be his anchor in the storm, and I want to be that person for Chad more than anything in the world. "I'm ready." Fake it till you make it, right? I can lose my composure once he's gone.

Hand in hand, we make our way into the hotel restaurant. Our friends and family are there, smiling and cheering. Chad pulls me into his arms and presses a kiss to my temple. We take the only two open seats that were saved for us and visit with those who are most important to us. We enjoy a nice meal, and to my surprise, everyone tells me they're sticking around for a few days to help me get settled. I smile and nod at this new information because words escape me.

I came to California to visit the man I gave my heart to, my best friend, and here I am—not two weeks later—his wife and getting ready to make a home for us. I'm also getting ready to send the man, my best friend and my husband, off for deployment.

No matter where he is in the world, one thing is certain. He'll be taking my heart with him, even if he doesn't know it.

Chapter 13

Chad

"**S**O I THINK THIS IS THE PART WHERE I TELL YOU IF YOU HURT my sister, I'll kill you."

I snort, my eyes completely focused on my wife across the table as she visits with Shayne and Cassie.

My wife.

I wasn't sure I'd ever hear those words when referring to Faith, but I'm damn glad I do.

"This is a little surprising, Chad, even for you." When I look his way, he continues, "Not that I'm knocking it, really. I'm just surprised. The last time we talked about Faith, you kept insisting you two were only friends. You didn't want to drag a relationship around with you while you did your job, wherever that would take you."

"I know what I said," I counter with a little extra irritation. "But I don't know, man. I just… love her." I tell her regularly, but I don't think she understands the true extent of it.

"And I get that too. It's funny how much your life changes when you find love."

I glance his way, even though I know his line of sight is exactly where mine was moments ago. Well, not exactly. He's looking at Shayne, the softest smile playing on his lips. "Have you two set a date?"

He nods. "We actually just decided on the plane ride over here. You've got seven months to complete your deployment and get your ass back home. I'm not doing this without you by my side."

A lump forms in my throat. "I'd be honored."

He looks my way and holds my gaze for a few seconds before replying, "It wouldn't be right without you, so get your time off request in now."

Chuckling, I reply, "Yes, sir."

"Sir. I like that," he retorts. We held the same rank until I relocated to California, and I've never called him sir.

"Don't get used to it. I technically outrank you now," I tease with a grin.

"Semantics," he says with a casual wave of his hand.

Before I can reply, I watch as the two moms—mine and Faith's—approach her. She stands up and listens to whatever they're saying before looking my way. There's a hint of uncertainty in her gorgeous green eyes, and I don't like it. Quickly, I stand and head their way.

"What's up?" I ask, my hand wrapping around her waist and drawing her against my side.

"We were just telling Faith it's time for you two to retreat to your hotel room," my mom announces, a mischievous look on her face.

"And I told them it wasn't necessary," Faith quickly adds. "You're leaving tomorrow. This is the last night with your family before you go." There's no missing the sadness in her voice. It reaches into my soul and squeezes.

"It's very necessary. You two are just starting your lives together, and it should be celebrated," her mom, Beth, states with a slight blush.

My cock jumps eagerly in my pants at the thought of *celebrating*.

Just as I open my mouth, my mom says, "We're going sightseeing. We'd love to check out this beautiful small town where you'll both be making your home for a while." She turns to Faith, takes her hand in hers, and adds, "We want you two to have one night together before my son leaves. You both deserve that much. We'll be ready in the morning to accompany you to the base for the family farewell." My mom's eyes fill with tears, which she blinks away. "Until then, we don't want to see either of you."

"That's right," Beth chimes in. "Go. Enjoy your night together. Who knows, maybe we'll get a grandbaby out of it."

That seems to perk my mom up right away. "Oh! Wouldn't that be something?" she gushes, making Faith blush even more.

"All right, that's enough. I'm going to take my wife up to our hotel room and spend the evening with her," I state, taking her hand in mine and giving it a squeeze. "Let's all meet down in the lobby at 0500. That'll give us time to get you all checked in on the base and to the gathering point."

"Sounds good," my dad states.

It takes us a few minutes to say our goodbyes to everyone, but as soon as we do, I'm ushering my wife toward the elevator. I allow her to push the Call button, mostly because my hands are occupied. I have one wrapped around her right one and the other on her waist. My fingers dance across the material of her dress, needing to feel connected to her.

Anchored to her.

The moment we step inside the car, and she presses the button for our floor, the air turns thick with desire. A heavy hum races through my veins as I turn to face her. Slowly, I back her against the wall, pinning her in place. Her eyes darken with need, her breath quickening. She licks her lips, a simple action that causes my cock to harden fully.

Just as I move to kiss her, the elevator chimes with the arrival to our floor. As much as I'd love to take her in my arms and kiss the hell out of her, the elevator probably isn't the best place for that. With a little extra bounce in my step, I guide her from the car and down the hall to the room. I have the key card out and slide it over the handle as soon as we arrive, waiting impatiently for that damn light to turn green. It only takes a moment to change, but it feels like a lifetime. Especially because I know it's the only thing holding me back from being alone with Faith.

My wife.

We slip inside the hotel room, and the electricity crackles around us. I drop her hand and throw the key card onto the dresser before turning and staring. She's so fucking beautiful, she takes my breath away.

Faith clears her throat and fidgets with her hands. I can feel uncertainty rolling off her in waves. Reaching out, I take her hands in mine and bring them to my lips. "What's wrong?"

"Nothing," she quickly blurts before clearing her throat once again. "I'm just… I guess I'm a little nervous."

"Why?" I ask, sliding my mouth across the softness of her knuckles.

"Uhh, things are… different now," she all but whispers.

"The only difference is we're married now. We've been here before."

She nods, her eyes dilate as she watches me kiss her skin. As I turn her hands over, I hear her gasp as my tongue slips out and glides across the pulse-point on her right wrist.

"What do you want to do?" I ask, feeling her shudder as I slide my fingers up her palm and link them with hers.

"I don't… What do you want to do?" A nervous Faith is quite something. I've only ever known her to be direct and blunt, taking what she wants.

I stop what I'm doing and meet her gaze. "Honesty?"

"Always."

"I want to make love to my wife."

The softest whimper slips from her lips as I pull her toward me, wrapping my arms around her body and feeling her pressing against me.

"What do you want, Faith?" I whisper, my lips dancing close to the shell of her ear.

"I want that too."

My body simultaneously tightens with need and relaxes in relief. Leaning forward, I brush my mouth against hers, reveling in the moment. I release her hands and gently cup her cheeks, slowly sliding them up and into her hair. The long, dark brown locks slip through my fingers as I deepen the kiss. Our tongues glide together, and I can feel her gripping my dress shirt.

"Faith?" I murmur, refusing to pull my lips from hers.

"Yes?"

"You look absolutely stunning in this dress," I tell her, my thumb trailing down the slender column of her neck and leaving goose bumps in its wake. "But I can't wait to see it off you."

She giggles the sweetest sound. "Likewise. I've never seen you look better than you do in your dress blues," she informs me, reaching down and tugging the bottom of my shirt from my pants as I shrug out of my coat.

My cock jumps with the eagerness of a virgin.

When she reaches for the buttons on my shirt, I grasp her hands gently and bring them to my mouth for a kiss. "Let me savor this moment. If I'm not going to get to see you like this for up to six months, I'm going to need to create a lot of memories tonight, beautiful. I want to memorize everything."

She pulls back and stands there in her dress. "Do you want to do the honors, or shall I?"

My brain practically short-circuits. On one hand, I most definitely want to do the honors, but on the other, the thought of watching her take off her wedding dress—just for me—has me so hard, I can barely breathe.

Moving to the chair in the corner of the room, I take a seat and try to adjust the discomfort in my groin. I kick my feet up on the footrest, raise my eyebrows suggestively, and wave my hand. "Proceed." When she reaches for the zipper running along her side, I add, "Slowly, beautiful. Make it hurt."

As if understanding my request and knowing how difficult it's going to be for me to just sit and watch her undress, she grins widely and nods.

The release of the zipper is somehow louder than the drum pounding in my chest and the blood swooshing in my ears. My eyes are riveted to her side where she painstakingly slowly drops the zipper, revealing a sliver of her soft flesh. My dick jumps. It actually kicks, trying to get closer to her.

She slips the straps of her dress off her shoulders. Holding her chest, she slides her arms out of the straps and lets them hang. Then, she starts to shimmy out of the bodice, taking her sweet-ass time, just like I requested. Between the pounding in my chest and the pain in my groin, she's definitely achieving what I requested. Sitting here, not touching her, watching her undress, fucking hurts.

The dress slips past her magnificent tits, and thanks to the fact she's not wearing a bra, I get an eyeful instantly. A groan slips from my mouth, and I have to force myself to remain seated. Faith grins, a knowing, naughty little smirk, as she continues to push the dress past her hips and onto the floor.

"Fucking hell," I mutter, taking in the exquisite sight before me, as I run my hand down my face.

My wife is wearing nothing but a tiny white scrap of lace, one which barely covers her pussy.

She reaches down and steps out of her dress, giving me more than I bargained for. But it's like that every time. She's so much more than I anticipated, every step of the way. As she collects the white dress, she turns, giving me the perfect view of her bare ass. The image of her bent over, wearing nothing but a white thong, is one of the many recollections I'll carry with me in deployment.

One of the many I'll think about as I do my job in hopes of rushing back home to her.

"What do you think, Mr. Anthony?" she croons, her sultry voice dripping over my heated body like honey.

"Fucking beautiful. The most beautiful woman in the world," I tell her, feasting on the sight of her. "Come 'ere."

With a sexy little grin, she takes three steps my way.

"Leave the heels on," I insist, reaching for her hand.

She straddles my lap, her knees barely fitting between me and the sides of the chair. "Anxious to get to the good stuff, I see," she replies, grinding her pussy against my rock-hard cock.

"You're every man's wildest fantasy," I tell her.

Especially mine.

She leans forward and presses her mouth to mine. "I don't need to be every man's. Just yours."

My eyes burn with the heat of a thousand suns as I gaze at the only woman I'll ever love. When words finally cross my lips, they're hoarse and raspy. "I'm yours. Always."

Her mouth sears me, branding me with her touch instantly as my hands move to the globes of her ass. The kiss immediately turns ravenous. Her hands dive between us, grappling for my belt and ripping open my trousers. I can feel the heat of her pussy hovering over me, and any speck of control I once held on to flies straight out the window.

Somehow, I lift my hips, completely ignoring the bite of her heels digging into my legs as she lowers my pants enough to free my cock. Before I can sit back down, her hands are wrapped around me, fisting my dick, stroking gently.

"This wasn't what I had in mind for making love to my wife," I say through gritted teeth.

Faith shrugs her delicate shoulders. "Next time," she insists, pulling her panties to the side and slowly lowering herself onto me.

"Wait. Condom," I grumble.

She pauses when the head of my cock is wrapped in her tight, wet heat. "I'm on the pill, Chad. And I've been tested before for, you know."

A loud groan pulls from my gut as I close my eyes, trying to just breathe through the pleasure. "I'm clean too, baby. I swear. I'd never risk you."

"Then make love to me without anything between us."

That's all it takes to snap the last thread of my control. I thrust upward gently, filling her completely in one stroke. Our combined moans of pleasure fill the room and spur me on. With my hands on her hips, I pump, letting my body set the pace. Faith meets me stroke for stroke, grinding down on me and chasing her own release. Her pussy tightens, and I know she's close already.

Releasing my lips, she sits up and bounces. Fucking takes me on the ride of my life, leading me straight toward the edge of the mountain. I follow willingly too, ready to dive off the cliff into the unknown.

I'll go anywhere with her.

With her hands on my chest, I watch as her orgasm grabs hold. Her back arches, her eyes flutter closed, and her body tightens as she convulses around me. Her release washes over her, taking me right along with it. I grip her hips tightly and pump into her. I come hard, waves of euphoria slamming into me like the surf on the shore.

"Holy shit," Faith mutters, collapsing against my chest, trying to catch her breath.

My brain can't even properly form a response. All I can do is grunt.

"That was an interesting version of making love," she quips, kissing the underside of my chin.

My arms tighten around her, holding her close. "Anytime we're intimate like this, it's making love, beautiful. And later, when I'm eating you out, watching you suck my cock, taking you from behind and seeing your ass turn red from my hand… everything, *that's* making love too."

She shivers against me, her pussy convulsing around my dick. "Sounds like a long night."

"I plan on using every minute I have with you, love. I can sleep on the plane," I state, only feeling slightly guilty about my plan to keep her up all night.

She doesn't complain, though, just cuddles against me more. My hand slides down her sweaty back and traces the edge of her thong. Her very stretched, distorted thong that'll definitely need to be ditched after tonight.

"Where did you get this?" I ask, kissing her shoulder and still trying to slow my racing heart.

"At a little boutique near where I got the dress."

"I was pleasantly surprised. Feel free to shop there again. Though, maybe wait until I'm returning," I state, realizing I'm not at all joking. The thought of anyone else seeing her in a white, lace thong has me ready to fight.

We sit together, her smaller frame tucked securely around me, and just breathe each other in. After a few minutes, she murmurs, "My legs are starting to fall asleep."

Smiling, I kiss the top of her head. "This is gonna be messy."

Her giggle vibrates through me. "I think you're right."

"We'll definitely need a shower," I state, wishing my pants weren't around my knees right now. Otherwise, I'd just stand and take us to the bathroom.

A wicked gleam fills her eyes. "And then we can get dirty all over again."

She has no idea how much tonight—today, really—has meant to me. When I said my vows, it was with only her and our future together in mind. All I have to do is make it through the next handful of months, and then I get to come back to her. It's going to be hell, don't get me wrong, but knowing she's here, waiting for me, is all the inspiration I need to do everything in my power to make sure I return safely.

Tomorrow isn't guaranteed, but it's what will keep me moving forward.

Every day that passes is one more closer to her.

Trying not to get too far ahead of myself and committing to staying in the moment, I push all thoughts of what happens tomorrow out of my mind. I have one night with my wife, and I plan to use every second.

All sorts of naughty ideas fill my mind, and my chuckle is low and gravelly. "I'm looking forward to it, beautiful. Tonight, you're all mine."

Chapter 14

Faith

I'M STARING AT THE CLOCK, WATCHING, WAITING AS EACH NUMBER ticks by. In an hour, we have to be up and moving so that Chad can make it to the base in time for his departure. I've been dreading this since the moment he told me he had to deploy. My heart hurts, the ache a steady presence with every beat.

My husband wraps his arms around me and places a kiss on my bare shoulder. I snuggle into his embrace. I'm soaking up every touch, every breath of his against my skin. I want to be wrapped up with him until the very last second.

We're both wide awake. Afraid to miss a single minute of time together before he has to go. I was worried he'd be exhausted, but he's assured me it's a long journey to where he's going, and he can sleep on the plane.

I don't want this to end. I'm deliciously sore from making love to him throughout the night. We tried like hell to make memories that would last until he comes home.

I know he has to go and I have to be strong for him. I have to set up his home so that he has a place to come home to. I don't know what waits for us when he's back, but I know he needs this. He needed someone to come home to, and I'm glad I can be that person for him.

Hopefully, by the time his deployment is over, he'll love me as more than just his friend, and we can keep moving forward with our future together. I shouldn't be thinking about that right now, but it's hard not to when I'm enveloped in his arms. I can feel the love and the dread of leaving rolling off him in waves. Part of me thinks he might already care more about me than we've shared, but the other part knows it's wishful thinking and my own feelings of hopeful projection.

My heart tells me there's more to this, and I'm going to grip that feeling with both hands. I'm going to be the best damn Army wife out there. He needs this. I can't imagine what it's like for them to deploy.

My brother loathed the idea of continuing to leave Shayne behind. I want Chad to have his military career. I just want to be there with him while he lives out his dream. Besides, he's giving me mine. He's given me a home, benefits, and security to take my dream job across the country from my family. He's my biggest supporter, and I'm determined to be that same person for him.

"I don't want to leave you." His whispered confession has tears welling in my eyes. I blink them away quickly, not daring to let them fall.

Rolling over, I rest my hand against his cheek. "This is who you are. My husband is serving our country, and I couldn't be prouder of you."

"I've never dreaded my job more than I do at this moment." He leans forward and presses a gentle kiss to my lips.

"We've got this, Chad. I'll get you all moved, and settled, and I'll be here waiting for you when you get home."

"That's different," he replies. I can hear the awe in his voice. "Knowing I have a wife to come home to."

"Well, you'll be used to it by the time you get home."

"I don't know that I'll ever be used to the fact that you're my wife, Faith."

"This is your reminder." I lift his hand and place a kiss on his wedding band.

"I don't need that reminder. There isn't a single moment in a day where I'm not thinking about you."

My heart lurches inside my chest at his confession. I want to ask him if he thinks about Ford as much as he does me. We're just friends. Friends who apparently get married and make love for hours on end. I don't have the guts to say the words. Besides, this isn't going to be an easy conversation, and the numbers on the clock keep moving forward. We don't have time. I need to send my husband off with a clear head, and hopefully a full heart, with the anticipation of coming home to me.

His wife.

"I need to start getting ready." There's regret and pain in his voice. "I don't know that I can do it, Faith. I don't know that I can climb out of this bed and make myself leave you. I just got you. It's not even been twenty-four hours since I made you my wife."

The lump in the back of my throat grows. I swallow it back, fighting against my own emotions. "I'll be your wife, no matter where you are in the world."

"I need you to be my wife in my arms, in my bed. I fucking hate this. I hate that I have to leave."

This time, it's me who moves forward as I press my lips to his. "This is who you are. I know that, and so do you. Does it suck? Yes, it does. But you've got this. A few short months, and then you'll be right back here."

"Four to six," he mumbles.

"We can do that. Easy-peasy." I hope that my voice is as carefree as I'm trying to make it sound, when the reality is that I'm dying inside and I feel the exact same way, but I'm his support system. I need to make this easier for him. I can fall apart once his bus pulls away. I'll have our friends and family here to pick me up. Right now, he needs me to keep him moving. To show him that we've got this, and although it sucks and I'm going to miss him like a limb, we've got this.

He's got this.

I've got this.

Four to six months, and then forever.

We can do this.

"Come on, husband. Let's get you ready to go." I keep my tone light, even though my heart is heavy as I start to roll over, but he stops me. He moves to his back and pulls me on top of him.

"Five more minutes."

I don't get a chance to reply before his lips meld with mine. He kisses me so tenderly, so slowly, it brings tears to my eyes. I fight against them, not willing to let them fall. I can do that after.

We kiss for far too long and end up having to rush to get ready to leave. Luckily, Chad packed for his leave early. I was also able to slip a letter into his bag without him seeing. I wanted him to have a piece of home as soon as he reached his destination.

By the time we make it to the lobby, our family is waiting for us. Everyone is wearing their emotions on their sleeves, and I know I need to do something. This is hard enough on him as it is.

"Good morning," I say cheerily. Fake it until you make it, or in this case, until your husband's bus that's taking him across the world for deployment drives away.

Chad releases my hand from his tight grip and slides his arm around my waist. His lips press against my temple, and I don't need his words to know he's thanking me for breaking up the sorrow of the moment.

"How about after this, we go have breakfast?" I ask our families.

"That's perfect, sweetheart," my dad speaks up.

"Are we doing this here or when we get there?" Ford asks.

"Oh, come with me." I look up at Chad and offer him a smile, before taking his hand and leading us down the long hallway in the hotel.

"Faith? Where are we going?"

"Married less than a day and already questioning your wife," I tease. My voice wobbles, and I clear my throat. I will remain strong for him.

When we reach the door that has a closed for a private meeting on the door, I push it open and step inside.

"What are we doing?" Chad asks again.

"I called the hotel and set this up. I wanted us to have a private place to say our goodbyes." I shrug like it's not a big deal. I pretend like my heart isn't racing so hard it feels as if it might jump right out of my chest.

Chad frames my face with his hands, and his eyes bore into mine. The look is intense, and his eyes tell me everything he can't say.

Thank you.

I need you.

I don't want to go.

"My wife," he whispers. When his lips touch mine, I don't care that our families are standing behind us, watching. All I care about is the man in front of me, my husband. Giving him the best send-off we can, that's what matters. Keeping his spirits strong and reminding him of what's waiting for him on the home front.

That's my mission before he embarks on his own.

I step back and smile at my mother-in-law. "Sorry, I'll stop hogging him."

She shakes her head, tears in her eyes, offering me a watery, sad smile. I step away. Well, I try to. Chad's hand on my arm stops me.

"I need you close, baby." His words are low, only for me, and they send a thrill through me.

I'll be whatever he needs.

I nod and move to stand close to him. He laces his fingers with mine and gives his mom a one-armed hug. I try to pull my hand away, but Chad's hold is firm. Again, without words, he's telling me what he needs. So I stop trying to step away from my husband and instead, relish the feel of his hand in mine, as each member of our family steps forward to hug him and tell him to come home safe.

Ford is the last to approach us, and I have to look away. My eyes find Shayne's and she offers me a weak smile of encouragement. I pull in a deep breath and slowly exhale. I can do this. Just a little longer. I have to keep myself together just a little longer. Shayne's subtle nod tells me she knows I can do this, and that the minute I need her, she's there.

"Brother." Ford's voice cracks.

I have to bite down on my lip. The subtle taste of blood spreads against my tongue as I fight my battle with tears.

"Check in on her, will you?" Chad asks.

Closing my eyes, I fight against the burn of tears. He's worried about me. This man who is leaving his loved ones to serve his country, and his worry is for me. My husband is one of the greatest men I've ever known. The other three are in this room.

"Always. You take care of you."

"I have too much to fight for," he replies.

I don't know much about why he's being deployed. I don't know where he's going to be or what he's going to be doing. That's one of the hardest parts of him leaving. If something happens, I'm depending on the Army to notify us, or him… depending on the situation. Sure, I'll be able to call, text, and email when the service is available, but what if that service isn't available? I make a mental note to stock up on stamps and stationery. As soon as I have an address, I'm going to flood him with mail, just in case that's the only piece of home he gets while he's away.

I can hear their mumbled words, but I'm too busy fighting tears to hear what they're saying.

"We should head to base." Chad slides his arm around my waist. I force a smile and nod.

"We'll follow you there," Ford tells him. We got them clearance yesterday so that this morning would be as easy as possible.

Our group heads toward the parking lot. Chad opens my door for me, and I offer him another smile. He closes the door, and I suck in a deep breath and quickly exhale. Just a little longer. I can keep up this act just a little longer.

Once he's behind the wheel, he slides his hand to my thigh, and that's where it remains until we reach the base. The drive is quiet. There's nothing else to be said. We both know the other is hating every moment of this. Rehashing it is only going to make it worse, so we both choose to remain silent during the drive.

"I'll get your door, baby."

I want to argue that he doesn't need to, but again, I stay quiet and nod. I'm giving him whatever he needs. My door opens and his hand appears. I take it, stepping out of the car. I move out of the way so he can shut the door. I shriek when he spins me around and presses me up against the car.

"I'm going to fucking miss you. So damn much, Mrs. Anthony."

"Every second of every day." My voice is meek, and the sadness is evident in my tone. Chad kisses me, just a quick press of his lips against mine, way too quick if you ask me, before he pulls away. Taking my hand, he leads me toward the bus.

There are already other families gathered around saying their good-byes. I can feel the heaviness on my chest, as if the heaviness of this moment is weighing me down. The ache is so strong it hurts to breathe.

My parents are the first to step forward. Again, my husband refuses to let go of me as he hugs them one last time. Ford and Shayne are next, followed by his parents and sister. Once everyone has had their final round of hugs, Chad pulls me into him. He wraps his strong arms around me, and I can no longer hold on to the sob that breaks free from my chest.

He buries his face in my neck, and I can feel the slight tremble in his hold. I wrap my arms around his neck and hold on with everything I've got. I want him to feel this hug for days, weeks, and months from now when he's missing home.

I lose track of time as we stand anchored together. When he finally pulls back, it's only far enough so that I can see his eyes.

"I hate that I'm missing you start your dream career. I hate that you've barely been mine, and I have to leave you. I hate that you're left to set up our home on your own. I hate the pain I see reflected back at me in your eyes. I hate it all, but I love that you're my wife, Faith Anthony." He moves to rest his forehead against mine. "I love you, my beautiful wife. Don't forget that."

My heart pounds in my chest. It's racing so hard, I feel it might suddenly stop working altogether, then again, that could be because my husband is leaving. It could also be because he told me he loves me. The intensity of his words don't feel like he's talking to a friend.

"I love you, my husband," I reply, pushing all the other thoughts out of my mind. We're running out of time, and I need to stay in this moment with him.

His breath hitches, and I know my words have affected him, just as much as his affected me. "I don't know if I can walk away from you, Faith."

"You're not walking away from me. You're serving our country. You're doing your job. It's taking you away from home for a while, but you'll be back."

"It's not dangerous, more training than anything, but there are always risks," he tells me. It's more than I know he was supposed to or allowed to say, and I appreciate him giving me that.

"How do you feel about the color gray?" I blurt.

"What?" He laughs, which was my intention.

"For the master bedroom. A dark gray is what I'm thinking."

His lips are against mine, and I get lost in his kiss. "The only thing I care about is that you're sleeping in our bed," he says, pulling away. "And that's where you'll be when I get home."

"So needy. Is this how all marriages work?"

"Damn right, I'm needy. Only for you. Only for my wife."

A voice comes over the speaker in the waiting area, giving a two-minute warning before boarding.

Two minutes.

Not long enough.

"I'll call when I can, and I'll write, and email, and anything else I can do to communicate with you. If it's a few days before you hear from me, don't worry, okay?"

I nod. The tears are hot behind my eyes. My vision is blurry. I blink rapidly to clear my eyes. I need to see him clearly. I focus on his neck as he swallows hard.

"Faith."

My eyes snap up to his, only to see tears as he blinks them away. "This is just a notch of time. There is so much ahead of us."

"Four to six months." I smile.

"Every second I'm away from you, I'll be thinking about you." He raises my hand and places it over his heart. It's thumping wildly inside his chest, the rhythm matching my own. "Right here, baby." He taps his hand over mine that's still resting against his heart.

"I love you, Chad Anthony." I need to say the words. I don't want any regrets.

"I love you, Faith Anthony." Another quick kiss, and he drops our joined hands and takes a step back. His eyes remain locked on mine with every step he takes away from me. Stopping, he picks up his bag and tosses it over his shoulder.

I wave as I lose my battle with my tears. I can't hold them back a second longer. Chad notices and runs back to me. His hands cradle my cheeks, and he kisses me hard. "No tears, baby. I'm coming home to you."

"I'll be here," I assure him.

"Love you." He kisses my forehead, then turns and walks away. I'm immediately flanked by our families as we watch him stop at the door of the bus. He turns and waves, blowing me a kiss before disappearing onto the bus.

All too soon, all I'm able to see are blurry taillights as the bus disappears out of sight. I can hear our family asking me if I'm okay, but all I can do is stand here, letting the tears roll unchecked down my cheeks, wishing that the bus would come back. If I could get one more kiss, just one more hug.

"Come with me." I recognize Shayne's voice as she wraps her arms around me and leads me back to the car. The car my husband bought for me. A sob breaks free from my chest, and I know that this pain will linger until the day I can wrap my arms around him again.

Chapter 15

Chad

THAT SUCKED.

I knew it was going to be hard to leave her, but damn, I didn't know it would be *that* hard. Sitting in my seat on the bus, I tilt my head back and close my eyes. I can still see the tears in my wife's eyes.

My. Wife.

She hasn't even held the title for twenty-four hours, and I had to go. For the first time, I regret not hanging up my boots when Ford did. I could have stayed with her, and I wouldn't have to pretend that our being married gave her a chance at her dream. I could have asked her to marry me because she owns my fucking heart. No pretending. No pretense. I could have and would have moved anywhere she needed to go to follow her dreams.

Instead, I re-signed, and I'm on this bus headed to God only knows where, while my new wife is left to pick up the pieces of my life. Thankfully, our families were able to make it on short notice, and I know they'll take care of her, but fuck me, I want to be the man to take care of her.

She's mine. My wife. That's my job.

"How you holding up?" Erik asks me.

Lifting my head, I open my eyes to see him sitting next to me. Erik and I have gotten close since I moved here. Ford will always be my best friend, but Erik, he's quickly sliding into that spot too. "Probably the same as you. This fucking sucks."

"Yeah," he agrees.

My mind keeps taking me back to our wedding. Faith looked gorgeous. It's an image that will forever be engrained in my memory. "She was beautiful. I wish we had more time together before we had to go."

Erik chuckles. "Man, I was there. I saw her. It's good to see you like this. The love of a good woman helps with these deployments. It's nice to know what we have at home waiting for us."

Instantly, I can see what that would look like playing out in my mind. After a long day, Faith would be there waiting for me to get home. We could talk about our days, make dinner together, then I'd make love to her before falling asleep with her in my arms. Only to wake up and repeat that same process the next day, and the next.

I want that life. I want it to be more than just a fantasy in my mind.

"How do you not hate the job for taking you away from her?" I ask him. It's just another thought that keeps racing through my mind.

"Sometimes I do," Erik admits. "I'm torn between serving my country and being there for my wife. We're going to try for a baby. When I get home," he confesses. "I know it's hard because we could get called out at any time, but she wants a piece of me, a piece of us, you know? I know she gets lonely and misses me, but man, a big part of me wants her to have a piece of the two of us in case something happens. If there ever comes a time I don't get to come home to her, she'll always have a piece of us and the love we shared."

"Fuck off. Don't talk like that." My voice holds no malice, but the thought of not coming home to Faith feels like a knife twisting inside my chest. "We're going home to our wives, and we're making all the babies." I know that's his future, and I'm happy as hell for the two of them. As for me, the thought of Faith carrying our baby has my cock stirring, and this is *not* the time for that to happen.

I want babies with her.

Only her.

I have up to six months to work on a plan to keep her. This marriage is real to me. It's the most selfish thing I've ever done, and I plan to fight like hell to keep her.

Faith Anthony is mine.

My phone vibrates as we pull up to the airfield. Quickly, I check it. My heart squeezes when I see her name. I swiftly changed her contact information from Faith to My Wife. Not that I need the reminder, but I like seeing those two words on my screen.

> **My Wife: Just wanted you to know I'm thinking about you. Please be safe. Check in when you can.**

> **Me: I'm always thinking about you, wife. I'll be safe, because I have someone really important to come home to. We're getting ready to board. I'll be silent for a while, but I'll check in with you when I can.**

> **My Wife: We're heading to check out the house. Married housing just called and said it's available. I'll text you the address.**

> **Me: Thank you for taking care of that. I'm sorry to dump this on you.**

> **My Wife: Meh, I get to put Ford to work. It keeps him young.**

It's on the tip of my tongue to tell her that I love her. Not just love her as my best friend but love her because she's my entire world.

> **Me: You do that. I'll reach out when I can.**

I love you.

My Wife: I miss you already.

Me: I miss you too, baby.

I hate to stop texting her. I have to force myself to put my phone on airplane mode as we board our flight. I could have stood on that bus forever texting her, but that's not my reality. I have a job to do—a dangerous job, and although I love my family and have often felt guilty for leaving them, that guilt has never been stronger than it is right now.

I'm supposed to be lying in bed with her gorgeous body wrapped around mine as we plan our future as husband and wife. Instead, I'm headed to what I'm sure is going to be the hot as hell desert while she starts her new job, her new life, without me by her side.

This fucking blows.

Boarding the plane, I insert my earbuds and close my eyes. I don't want to talk to anyone, anyway. I want to sit in silence and pout because I miss my wife. I miss the feel of her soft skin and the taste of her lips against mine. I'm worried she'll forget what it feels like to be in my arms. I'm worried that she's going to build this new life that I'm not a part of.

It's going to be hard, but I'm going to write to her as much as I can, even if I can't mail them right away. I'm going to remind her every fucking day that she's my wife. Then, when I get home, we'll talk about forever, because that's what we are.

We're forever.

She just doesn't know it yet.

The desert.

It's dry and hot as fuck. We made it to where we're going to be for the next four to six months, and I've never missed home more. I'm trained for this. I knew what to expect, but to be here and be living it, that's altogether different.

We're set up in tents, with cots inside for when we get to sleep. There are long hours ahead of us. We have a command station tent that has a couple of computers and a few cell phones, but we're so far out, I don't know what kind of connection there will be. That knowledge has my heart racing. I can't go that long without communication with her. I can't do it.

"Hey, they said mail leaves and delivers once a week," Erik tells me. He tosses his bag on his cot that's next to mine and starts to unpack his belongings into the trunk at the foot of his cot.

"Once a week." I nod. "That's better than never."

"Yeah, that's seven days without hearing from them. Last time, Hannah wrote so many letters, I got a stack each mail day. I would save one a day, going in order of the postmarks just to feel like I have a new piece of her each day. I responded to every one of them in a separate letter in case she wanted to do the same."

I'm already nodding before he's even finished talking. "I like that idea. I'll do that too."

Lifting my bag up on the cot, I unzip to start unpacking, and a white envelope catches my attention. I pull it out, and stare at the handwriting that's undeniably my wife's.

Turning, I sit down on the bed and stare at the envelope. I don't know why, but I lift it to my face and inhale deeply, trying to catch her scent. It smells like her. Closing my eyes, I can almost feel her sitting next to me.

"I got one too." Erik holds up his envelope.

My voice is thick when I reply. "Our wives—they're something else."

"I'm glad they have each other while we're gone."

"Yeah," I agree.

"I think I'll take a walk to read mine."

I think I reply, but I can't be sure. Instead, I block out every single thing around me, except for the letter I'm holding in my hands. Carefully, I open the envelope and pull out the white sheet of paper and start to read.

Chad,

You're not gone yet, and I already miss you. Tomorrow is our wedding day, and I wasn't sure if I'd find the time to write this, so here I am. I'm sitting in our hotel room, and I have so much I want to say but can't seem to find the words.

When you asked me to come and see you, I never could have imagined that we'd end up being married, and you being deployed, all within a matter of two weeks. It's almost scary how fast life can change, and plans can be derailed.

Although, I admit, I'm not mad about this derailment. I've accepted my dream job, and it's just a few short months. Okay, well, half a year at most, and you'll be home.

I can do that.

My plan is to throw myself into my work so that maybe I won't miss you as bad. It sounds good when I say it in my head, but reading it as I'm writing it, I know that nothing will keep me from missing you. Nothing except for you being here with me.

I guess I should warn you to expect a lot of letters. I want you to have as much of home with you while you're away as I can. I want you to feel like you're here with me.

I want to feel like you're here with me.

Please know that I'll miss you every second of every day.

Come home safe. Come home to me.

I can't wait to marry you tomorrow.

Always,
Faith

My hands clutch the letter as if it were her. I'm not ready to let her go just yet, so I read the letter twice more, before folding it neatly, and placing it back in the envelope. I check the reception on my cell phone and there's nothing in this tent. I hope there is somewhere here where I can get a signal to call her. If not, looks like I'll be in the common tent with everyone else trying to connect with their families. Digging inside my bag, I find my notebook and envelopes and immediately write her back.

My wife,

I hate that I had to leave you so soon. I regret that we didn't have more time together. I miss you too. So much, in fact, I can feel the ache in my chest. Thank you for your letter. Holding it felt as though you were here with me. It was almost as if you were giving me one final hug.

I keep seeing images of you this morning when you woke up in my arms. Your hair was a mess, and you didn't have a speck of makeup on, and all I could think about was how beautiful you were. How lucky I am to call you mine. I am you know, I'm the luckiest man on the planet. I'll never forget what it was like to wake up with you in my arms, knowing you were my wife.

I miss you so damn much.

We made it to where we're going. It's hot as hell, and nothing but sand for miles. I'll reach out to you every chance I get. If I go silent for a few days, know that I'm always thinking of you. I don't know how good the reception is here. From the looks of where we are, it's not real promising.

Mail runs once a week, so if my letters are delayed, you'll know why.

I need to unpack, but I had to reply to your letter first. Finding that letter in my bag was exactly what I needed. Married for a day, and you're already taking care of me. Is this what I have to look forward to for the next sixty years?

All of my love,
Chad

I read over my words and hesitate when I get to the last paragraph, but I decide to go with it. I won't tell her how I really feel in a letter. I won't do that unless I think there is a chance I won't make it back home to her. However, I'm not going to hold back either. I need her heart just as invested as mine.

I need her to be mine for more than just this deployment. A lifetime with Faith won't be long enough. Folding the paper, I stuff the envelope and address it with the one she sent me, anxious to get it in the mail. It's still hard for me to believe that I get to call her mine.

Quickly, I unpack, shoving my bag beneath my cot and head off in search of cell reception. From the time change, I know it's late in California, but I need to hear her voice. I walk about a hundred yards from where we're staying and get my first line of signal. I stop walking and dial her number, hoping the call goes through.

She picks up on the first ring. "Chad."

My body relaxes. The tension rolls away at the sound of her voice. "How's my wife?"

She laughs.

Fuck, I wish I could bottle that sound.

Maybe I can ask her to do a voice recording and send it to me. Hearing her laugh would definitely help get me through what's to come while we're here.

"Exhausted. We moved everything from the hotel to the house. It's so cute, a two-bedroom. It almost looks like a cottage."

"Is everyone still there?"

"Ford and Shayne are here. They're in the guest room on an air mattress they picked up in town. Our parents all went back to the hotel, and your sister too. I offered her to sleep with me in our bed, but she said someone had to keep our parents in line." She chuckles, as if the thought of our parents causing trouble is hilarious, and it is. I'd be laughing too, but I'm stuck on her saying "our bed," and wishing like hell I'd had a few more days, hell, months, to be with her before I had to deploy.

"That's good. I'm glad you're not alone. How is the house? Is it in decent shape?"

"Yeah," she replies softly. "It's really cute, actually. The previous tenants left some furniture. It's nothing fancy, but I like it. How are things?"

I spend a few minutes telling her about the hot desert sun, the dry sand, and our living conditions. "It's not home," I tell her. What I don't say is that even living in this dust bowl, if she were here, it would feel like home.

She's my home.

"Did you get my letter?"

"I did. Thank you. It was exactly what I needed."

"Good, because I might have already written you another one."

"Read it to me."

"What? No. I'm going to put it in the mail in the morning."

"I wrote you back, too, but we only get incoming and outgoing mail once a week."

"Well, I guess that means you're going to be getting a lot of letters on mail day."

"Good. It makes me feel close to you."

"Read it to me." She tosses my words back at me. "Oh, and thank you for the stack of envelopes."

"I did that while you were gone. I had some nervous energy. It made me feel like I was doing something to help you prepare to leave. There are some in your bag that are blank, with just stamps as well. I'll send you more in my package next week."

"You don't have to send me anything."

"I'm your wife; of course I do."

My. Wife.

I love saying it. I love hearing it, but hearing it from her lips, that does something to me. Something that has my pulse racing. I've always wanted her. From the moment we met, she was the only woman I could see. Now she's mine, and I'll be damned if I let her go without a fight.

"I should let you get some sleep. I'm exhausted, and I need to report in thirty minutes to get our orders."

"Please stay safe."

"Always."

"I miss you."

"I miss you too. I'll call again when I can."

"Okay." I can hear the crack in her voice. I want to tell her not to cry for me, but I can feel those same emotions welling inside me too. The pain of being away from her is almost too much to bear.

"Bye, baby."

"Bye."

My hand shakes as I force myself to remove the phone from my ear and end the call. I slide my phone into my pocket and head back to the tent. The sooner I get my assignment, the sooner this starts, and I can get home to her. I'm hoping for four months, not the six they say is possible. Four months is too long, and six seems like a lifetime.

Chapter 16

Faith

WALKING OUT OF THE BEDROOM, I SMILE WHEN I SEE THE picture from our wedding day hanging on the wall. I look at it every single day. I was able to get prints made before Ford left and he made sure to hang it for me. Not that I couldn't handle it on my own; it's not rocket science. However, my brother spouted off something about little sisters and best friend's wives. I didn't quite understand his mumble, but I got the gist of it. He was taking care of me, not only because I was his little sister, but because I was his best friend's wife.

I'm somebody's wife.

That's hard to grasp most days. The ceremony feels as though it was a dream. In fact, if it hadn't been for both of our families hanging around a few extra days to help me move into this house and get settled, it would be hard for me to grasp. I guess there is also the wedding band on my left hand, one that I look at often, and then the photo hanging on the wall.

Not just the wall. I bought some frames, and I have them all over the house. The nightstand, one on the kitchen counter, the living room, and I even considered one in the bathroom, but decided that was a little too far. I wanted to be able to see him everywhere. That was my goal, and I accomplished it. I'm sure when Chad gets home, he'll want to change that, but for the next few months, this is our home, one where I want a constant reminder of my husband.

Chad has been gone for two weeks. Our families are back to their lives, and I'm here on my own. I'm so thankful for Hannah and her friendship. We make it a point to have dinner together a couple of nights a week. I don't feel so alone with her around. Life is moving forward, and that is both exciting and heartbreaking. I miss him more than I thought possible. I missed him when he was gone before, but this… this feels different. This time he's my husband.

I miss my husband.

I've written so many letters that I'm worried he's going to get tired of hearing from me, but I want him to feel as if he were here. Not only that, but I also want to share this part of my life with him. Today, I start my new job, and I wrote him a letter last night telling him all about it. When he comes home, I want it to feel as though he's only been gone a few days, not months.

Glancing at the clock, I realize I've sat here too long thinking about Chad, about missing him. I'm going to be late for my first day. I quickly rinse out my coffee cup and place it in the sink to handle when I get home tonight. With one more quick glance at our wedding photo, I grab my bag and head to work.

"Good morning, class. I'm Mrs. Anthony." My smile is huge because nineteen little humans are giving me their full attention. I'm a kinder-garten teacher. I get to help shape their minds and be their first real experience with learning in the school system outside of preschool. Half of my students didn't attend preschool from what their records show. My smile might also be that I'm Mrs. Anthony. Yeah, that's a big part of it.

"We're going to go around the room, and I want you each to tell me your name. When I tap your shoulder like this—" I tap my own shoulder, and they giggle "—that's when it's your turn." I make my way down the aisles of their tables and tap each child on the shoulder. For some, I have to help coax them to speak, and for others, well, I have to remind them that their classmates need a turn as well.

By the end of the day, we're all exhausted, but it feels incredible. This is what I went to school for. Kindergarten has always been my dream, and I'm living it thanks to my husband. I take my time cleaning up the classroom in preparation for the next day before heading home.

As soon as I walk into the house, my eyes go to the wedding photo. "Hey, babe," I greet. It sounds crazy talking to a picture, but it makes me feel closer to him. Besides, it's just me here. There is no one to cast judgment.

Leaving my stuff on the couch, I move to the bedroom to change into something more comfortable before moving back to the kitchen. I'm standing with the refrigerator door open, trying to decide what to eat for dinner, when my cell phone rings. I freeze, trying to remember where I dropped my stuff, and sprint toward the living room.

It's been two weeks since I've heard his voice. I usually have my phone with me at all times. The one time I don't, I get a call. Sure, I don't know if it's him, but I don't want to miss him if it is.

I scramble with my bags, shoving my hands into my purse to find my phone. I grab it and see his name. My hands shake as I hit Accept. "Chad."

"What's wrong?" There's concern in his voice.

I huff out a laugh as I plop down on the couch. "Nothing. I was in the kitchen. I've been keeping my phone with me, and the one time I didn't, it rang, and I rushed to answer it."

"Sounds like you miss your husband." His tone is much lighter.

"You could say that." The refrigerator beeps with its annoyance for being open too long, so I stand and rush to close it. "How are you?"

"I'm better now that I'm talking to you. I got a big stack of letters today."

"Yeah, sorry about that."

"What? Why are you apologizing? I want to hear from you."

"That's good; I've mailed one, sometimes two, a day since you've been gone."

"Good. I want to be a part of your life, Faith."

I glance at our wedding photo on the wall. "You are." I pause, collecting myself. I don't want him to hear the sadness in my voice. He's the one who's away from home, potentially risking his life for his country. I'm supposed to be his solid foundation, and I'm going to be. "Tell me everything."

He laughs. The sound is rich, and I can tell it comes from a place deep inside his chest. "Lots of sand, and lots of heat. Long days, and even longer nights."

"But you're safe?"

"Yeah, baby, I'm safe."

My heart melts at the way he calls me baby. "I have a care package to send to you tomorrow."

"You don't have to do that."

"Come on now. What kind of wife would I be if I didn't send care packages to my husband? Is there anything you want or need? Anything nonperishable you've been craving?" I ask.

"Nah, I think we're still set."

"Then you'll just be surprised, I guess."

"A surprise from my wife sounds like exactly what I need. How was your first day?"

Tears spring to my eyes. He remembered. He's thousands of miles away in the desert, but he made it a point to find the time to call and ask about me first.

"Good." I clear my throat. "I'm exhausted, but in a good way, you know? This is what I thought my teaching career would look like. It's... incredible to know that I'm finally starting my career the way I'd always hoped."

"That's good to hear. I'm glad it went well."

"Very. My fellow teachers are friendly. I love my classroom. I took a few pictures. I emailed them, but I'm not sure if they went through."

"I haven't checked. Service is spotty, and so far, I've only found this one location that I can get a connection to call. I was lucky that my shift is tonight, so that I would be up to call you to ask about your day."

"The only thing that would have made it better is if you were here to celebrate it with me. Instead, Hannah and I are having dinner on Friday night."

"I'm glad you have her."

"I'm glad I have you."

"It's different this time," he confesses. "My deployment."

"How so?" I have a thousand ideas running through my mind about what he might say. That it's more dangerous, hotter, more work, just to name a few.

"Because I know I have you, my wife, waiting at home for me. We always do our best to take the most safety precautions we can. However, now, it's even more important. Outside of my immediate family, I've never had anyone at home waiting for me."

"You have me. I'm your family now." I want to be his home, because he is mine. It's no longer a place, it's Chad.

"I know you are, baby. That's what makes this different. I've never resented my job, not a single day since I signed up. Not until I had to walk away from you and step on that bus, not even twenty-four hours after you became my wife."

"I wish you were here."

"I am there. Maybe not physically, but I'm with you, Faith. Always." He sighs heavily, and I know that means our time is over. "I need to go. I just wanted to hear about your day and hear your voice."

"You made my day better than I could have imagined." It's true. This day was already perfect, but him calling made it exceptional.

"I'll call soon."

"Be safe."

"I love you." Those three words mean something altogether different to me than they do him, but I repeat them anyway.

"I love you too."

The line goes dead, and it feels as though my heart is splintering in two. I love talking to him, to get to hear his voice, but when he has to go, it's just like he's stepping onto that bus all over again.

"I'm stuffed." I push my plate away from me. It's Friday night, and Hannah and I are having dinner.

"Me too," Hannah says, doing the same. "We'll get two boxes and split the leftovers. Cold pizza for breakfast is life." She laughs and takes another sip of her wine.

"The food was great, but it's even better that this place is within walking distance for both of us, and this"—I hold up my glass of wine—"this is just what we needed."

Hannah clicks her glass against mine. "Yeah, but you know what I miss?"

"Erik?" I state the obvious.

"Yeah, Erik and sex."

My mind instantly goes to my wedding night. "Yep," I agree. If I were to close my eyes right now, I could picture him moving above me. His gaze never leaving mine as he thrusts inside me. I squirm in my seat, pressing my thighs together. Is it cliché to say that my wedding night was hands down the best sex of my life?

"I send him pictures," she confesses.

"What?" My mouth falls open. "Like sexy pictures?" I whisper, not wanting the families that are eating a few booths over to hear our conversation.

She nods. "He sends them back."

I'm not sure what to say. Partly because all I keep thinking about is sending a couple to Chad and what his reaction might be. "The service is spotty." It's a lame reply, but I'm still processing. I would never have considered it, but now it's all that I can think about.

"It is, but when he gets service, it's a nice surprise. We gotta do what we gotta do while our husbands are gone. You should consider it."

I'm nodding. "I should try it."

Her grin is wicked. "Do it. He's going to be shocked, but he's going to love it."

"You think?"

"Faith, they're in the middle of the desert. They have nothing but sand and heat. Of course he's going to love getting images of his wife in a—" She looks around us and then turns her eyes back to me. "—compromising position."

"Okay."

She grins and slides out of the booth. "It's on me tonight. You, my friend, need to go home and have a photoshoot."

"Do you dress up?" I ask, placing the tip on the table, and following her to the register. I'm out of my depth here. I have no idea where I would even start, but the idea, it's taking root and I want to try. I want to do that for him.

"Sometimes, but he doesn't care either way. It's me, and when he's missing me, that's all that matters."

I wonder if Chad is missing me like that. Either way, I've made up my mind. I'm doing this. I want to be his wife in every way when he's deployed and when he's home. This is a part of that. I want to take care of him while he's gone.

Hannah hugs me on the sidewalk in front of our house. She and Erik live just a few more houses down. "Let me know how it goes." My face flushes beneath the streetlights and she laughs. "I don't need details, and I'm certain he'll love it, but you can give me confirmation."

Instead of answering her, I pull her into another hug. "Thank you for dinner. Next week it's on me."

"Sounds like a plan. Have a good night." She winks.

"You too." I laugh, because it's weird that she knows what I'm about to do. Unlocking the front door, I turn on the small lamp in the entryway. Making sure the door is locked, I toss my keys and purse on the small kitchen island, and with my phone clutched in my hand, I move toward the bedroom.

I don't own sexy lingerie. Something I'll remedy if this goes over well. So tonight, he's just getting me. Quickly, I strip out of my clothes and wash my face. I'm just me. I know he likes this. He told me so in one of his letters. Easing back on the bed, I hold the phone above my head and take a few shots. I scroll through them, and they're okay, I guess. I'm not really sure what I'm going for because I've never done this.

I settle on one that shows my face. I'm staring at the camera, and my eyes are hooded. My bare breasts are on display, my hard nipples making themselves known. Before I can change my mind, I pull up our message thread.

Me: Missing you.

I attach the image and hit Send.

Tossing my phone onto the mattress, I stare up at the shadows on the ceiling. I never in a million years would have thought that sending a sexy picture would turn me on so much. I think it's more of the fact that he's going to see it. I wish I were there so I could see his face.

Cupping my breasts, I tug at my nipples, causing a moan to fill the silence of the room. Closing my eyes, I picture our wedding night. I pretend like it's his hands roaming over my body. My hand finds its way to my aching clit.

I need the release.

I'm wet just from the thought of my husband. I wonder if he'd want to see that. See what he does to me, living thousands of miles away.

Without allowing myself to overthink what I'm doing, I spread my legs, reach for my phone and snap a picture. I'm not sure if it will come out, but when I glance at the screen, my breath hitches. The evidence of my arousal is obvious, even with the darkness of the image.

I dip my fingers inside, and my back arches off the bed. It's not going to take long. I imagine that it's my husband's expert yet calloused hands bringing me pleasure, and I detonate like a rocket. I'm panting, trying to catch my breath, and when I do, I snap another picture. I don't think as I type out another message.

Me: This is all for you.

I send the before and after picture of my arousal. It's the most daring thing I've ever done, but it feels right sending them to Chad. To my husband. I know he would never share those images. Even when he's not here, he's my protector. I feel that with everything that I am.

Rolling out of bed, I move to the bathroom and get cleaned up before plugging my phone in to charge and sliding beneath the sheets. I'm smiling as I drift off, thinking of my husband's reaction when he gets his messages. I also wonder if he'll send me an image back. I hope it doesn't take another two weeks. Regardless, they'll be there for him when he gets service.

He'll know I was thinking about him.

I'm always thinking about him.

Chapter 17

Chad

THE DAYS ARE LONG, AND THE NIGHTS ARE LONGER. ONCE THE sun goes down, the temperature takes a drastic turn. While it's incredibly hot during the day, the sand absorbs the heat rapidly and the air becomes very cool. We go from sweating our balls off to needing warm clothes.

It's miserable.

It's not my first time being in this type of climate, but it's the first time I know there is something infinitely better waiting for me at home. I miss my wife, and I would give anything to be curled up next to her right now. We just got back to camp. I need a shower and some food, and if I'm lucky, I can rush through both and call Faith. It's been over a week since I've heard her voice.

Inside the tent, I make my way to my cot and can't stop my grin when I see the mail run today. It was supposed to be here two days ago, but there was a delay. Taking a seat, I eye the stack of letters and a box.

I want to open it all at once, but I start with the letters. I check the post-mark and open them in order.

"Mail day," Erik says, plopping down on his cot, and going through his stack. I tune him out. I tune everything out but Faith.

The first is a thicker envelope, so I carefully tear it open, assuming there's something inside. Once the seal is broken, I reach in and pull out two thin pieces of cardboard and an envelope. I check between the cardboard first, and my breath hitches at what I see.

Wedding photos.

My hands shake as I sift through the images she sent me. I miss her so fucking much. I hate being away from her. What I hate even more is that she doesn't know, not really. She doesn't know that she owns me. She doesn't know that when I tell her that I love her, it's more than just loving my friend. I love her in all the ways a husband should love his wife.

Probably more.

When I reach the last picture, my breath hitches. It's Faith all on her own, but there's a satisfied smile pulling at her lips. My eyes scan her features. She's looking off into the distance, and that's when I realize what or who she's looking at.

Me.

She's looking at me.

The smile on her face is full of love and happiness, and she's looking at me. My heart feels like it might be too big for my chest. It's the look that tells me this is more for her too. I'm not in this alone. This isn't temporary for either one of us. I have to force myself to set the pictures aside and open her first letter.

Chad,

I spent the entire day setting up my classroom. I have the seating chart made and my students' names in their places. By the time they're moving on to first grade, they will be able to read simple words and sentences. I have this giddy feeling that I can't seem to shake. They're going to learn all of that because of me. I get to help shape their little minds. It's a rush.

Anyway, I'm home now, and the house is quiet. Everything is unpacked, and I've ordered a few items online to make it feel more like home. A few picture frames, some pillows, and a throw blanket for the living room. I'm trying to make them more masculine so that when you get home, you won't feel like you're living in just my space. I want it to be ours.

Tomorrow is my first day with students, and I wish you were here. I'll be sure to write to you and tell you all about it.

I hope things are well with you, and you're staying safe. I miss you. I would give anything to have your arms wrapped around me in a hug right now.

Love,
Faith

I need to read the rest of her letters, but first, a shower. I have sand in places sand should never be, and I'm starving. I have just enough time to grab a shower and get to the mess hall tent before calling her. Tucking the letters away, mindful of the pictures, I place them in the trunk at the end of my cot, along with the box. I'm sure it's filled with goodies from home, and if I'm lucky, it will smell like her.

I miss her smell. I miss her touch. I just fucking miss her.

An hour later, I'm showered as best as I can be, considering our amenities. Anything is better than nothing at this point. My belly is full, and with my cell phone clutched in my hand, I'm headed toward my spot to get service to call her. I need to hear her voice.

As I'm walking to my hot spot, as I like to call it, I power my phone on. I keep it off to save the battery. There's no point in leaving it on if I don't get service, so that cuts down on how often I need to charge it. I'm probably ten steps away from where I usually stop when my phone pings, telling me I have new messages.

I scroll through the screen and see one from Ford. My mom and dad both sent messages, and my little sister too. Then I see the name I long to hear from. *My Wife.* I stop walking and open her messages. I freeze when images of her fill the small screen.

"Fuck me," I mutter as I lift the phone closer to my face to make sure my eyes aren't deceiving me. Sure enough, it's not a mirage caused by the desert heat. My wife has sent me pictures of her.

Naked pictures.

Not just naked but aroused. She's wet. I can see the evidence even in the dim lighting of the image of her glistening pussy. My cock is hard and straining against my pants. She's so damn sexy. The thought of her touching herself, thinking about me, it's almost more than I can take.

With a power I didn't know I possessed, I lift my eyes from the screen and scan the area. Nothing but desert. There is no shelter, but I'm up here all alone. I've told Erik about this spot, but he knows I'm up here, so he'll take his turn after. With my back facing camp, I unzip my pants and pull out my cock. It's hard and weeping for my wife. I stare at her pictures on the screen, flipping through them with one hand, while choking my cock with the other.

I need her.

I'm so desperate for relief that it doesn't matter if I get caught. The pictures don't do her justice, but it's as close as I can get to the real thing. Or is it? I quickly calculate the time difference. It's Friday night, and just after ten her time. It's a dick move calling this late, but I need her. She doesn't work tomorrow, so she can sleep in. I'm ready to hit Call but hit the option for Video Call instead. I hope that the reception is good enough for the connection to be clear.

"Chad?" she answers.

I watch the screen as she sits up. She's wearing one of my Army T-shirts. The image of her has my cock twitching in my palm. "Hey, baby." I smile at her.

She reaches over to turn on the lamp, and I can now clearly see her. Her hair is pulled up in a messy knot on top of her head, and her face is free of makeup. This moment reminds me of waking up with her in my arms for the first time as my wife. A moment I'll never forget, and I'm sure this one will be added to that list as well.

"Hi." Tears fill her eyes.

"Faith." I breathe her name. "I got your messages." Her face flushes. "I needed to see you."

"Yeah, it's good to see you too."

"You have no idea what you do to me. I'm standing beneath the desert sun with my cock in my hand, thinking of you."

"Are they okay?"

"Are they okay?" I huff out a laugh. "They're more than okay. They're unexpected and sexy, and my mouth is watering. Seeing your pussy glistening like that, I can almost taste you on my tongue."

"I wasn't sure. Hannah said that she sends pictures to Erik, and I know it's lonely, and since we're married, I mean, it's not like it's something you've never seen before."

"I only want to see you."

She's quiet for a few seconds, and I let the silence linger between us as I squeeze my cock at the base. "She said he sometimes sends them back—pictures, I mean. Of him, not of her," she rambles.

She's nervous, but she shouldn't be. Not with me. "Faith?"

"Yeah?"

"You're my wife. That gives you the right to ask me anything. Tell me what you want." I know what she wants, but I want to hear the words fall from her sweet lips.

"I'd like to have images of you too. I have wedding pictures, but… that's not the same."

"You want to see my cock, wife?"

She nods. "Only my husband's."

"Fuck." I curse under my breath. Panning the phone, I show her my cock fisted in my palm. "Like this?" I ask. I can't see the screen very well. There is a glare from the sun at this angle, but I hear her intake of breath.

"You—I wasn't sure if you were exaggerating."

"Never. You get my truth always. This is what your pictures did to me."

"Can I watch you?"

I huff out a laugh. "That's why I called you."

"But I want pictures too."

"Is my wife greedy? Does your pussy ache for me?"

"Please."

"Please, what?" I know what she wants. I want it just as badly, but I need to hear her ask for it. I don't know why, but not being there and hearing her tell me what she needs from me makes me feel as though I'm taking care of her. I always want to take care of her.

"Show me."

"Get naked." I move the phone back to a position where I can see her. She tosses off the covers and pulls my T-shirt over her head. She stands, placing her phone down on the bed. I can hear her moving as she strips out of her panties. When she picks the phone back up, she's lying on the bed. Her hair is splayed out over the pillow, and her eyes are filled with desire.

"There she is." I smile at her. "Baby, I'm close. It's not going to take much for me, so we need to get you there."

"Tell me what you want me to do."

"Pinch your nipple. Pretend like it's my teeth grazing the hard bud."

She does as I ask, a slight moan filling the air.

"Good girl," I praise. "I wish I could taste them. Fuck, Faith, my mouth is craving your soft skin beneath my tongue."

"Yes."

She's lost in the moment. "I need your fingers in your pussy, baby. I need you to pretend like they're my cock."

"Oh, God," she cries out as her hand slides over her belly.

"Move the phone."

"I can't see you."

"You first, wife. Always you first." She does as she's told and moves the phone. I watch as her thumb gently rolls over her clit. "How does it feel?" I ask her.

"Sensitive."

"Let me see." She moves the phone even lower, and without being told, slides her index finger through her wet pussy. I can see her arousal, but I can also hear it. My cock is leaking. I'm so turned on. I don't know how much more I can take. "Two fingers," I grit out. "It's me inside you, remember?" I tell her.

"Only you."

"That's right, wife. Only me. Faster." I watch the screen as she plunges two fingers in and out of her pussy. I squeeze my cock, trying to hold off. I want us to come together, but it's only fair she gets to watch me too.

"C—Chad," she moans.

"I'm here," I tell her. "I'm right fucking here, and I can see you, Faith. I see the way your hand is thrusting inside my pussy. I see the evidence of how wet you are with each glide of your fingers. I can fucking hear it."

"I—I'm going to come."

"Good girl. Come for me, my wife. Show me how much you miss me. I want your hand soaked, just like mine is about to be." That does it. She calls out my name, and her back arches off the bed. Her hand doesn't stop until she's ridden the full wave of the ecstasy rolling through her veins.

I'm desperate for relief. "Baby, I need to see you."

She groans but pulls the phone to her face. Her cheeks are flushed, her eyes are hooded, and she's the most beautiful fucking woman I've ever laid eyes on. "You with me?"

"Yeah. It's your turn, husband," she whispers.

"Holy fuck. Why is that so hot? You calling me your husband?" I pan the phone to my cock. "Can you see?" The desert sun is glaring down on me as I stroke myself.

"Every inch."

Jesus. I take the cum that's leaking to help my hand glide. I stroke from root to tip, squeezing, trying to mimic what it feels like when I'm at home inside her.

"I don't know what to say. How can I help you?"

"You're breathing."

"What?"

"All you have to do is breathe, baby. You're sexy as fuck and just gave me hours and hours of spank bank material. I just need to hear you breathe."

"Does it hurt?"

"Yes, but not how you're thinking."

"Tell me." There's a plea in her voice. She needs to hear me say it just as bad as I did.

I'm desperate for release, not conversation, but I'll never deny her anything. "It hurts that it's my hand and not your pussy. It hurts that I don't get to feel my fingertips glide over your smooth skin. It hurts that I'm standing here beneath this scorching sun when all I want to do is be wrapped around you in our bed. It hurts because I miss you so fucking much."

"I miss you too."

We're both quiet, so I close my eyes and get back to business. My cock is swollen and painful. I need this release.

"Does your hand feel like my pussy?" Her words are whispered, but she might as well have screamed them for the effect they have on me.

"No. Nothing feels as good as your hot, wet heat wrapped around me."

"My mouth. I think my mouth would be a good second."

"Jesus fuck, baby." I can feel the tingling in my spine. My balls tighten, and I stroke faster. Squeeze a little harder, chasing my release.

"I could come again just watching you."

Her words have their desired effect. I call out her name as I shoot off my release. I'm a mess. My hand, my shirt, hell, even the sand got a heavy dose of my desire for my wife. With no other options, I tear off my shirt and clean up. I know that I'm lucky I didn't get caught, so I quickly tuck myself back into my pants and zip up.

"I can't believe we just did that," she says. There is a smile and, if I'm not mistaken, a little bit of awe in her voice.

"You've created a monster," I tell her. Already thinking about when I can call her again.

"Chad?"

"Yeah, baby?"

"I didn't get any pictures."

I toss my head back in laughter. "I'll make sure you get your picture. Right now, my cock is sated, but I promise you, I'll get them to you."

"You always keep your promises."

"Always," I say as she covers a yawn. She's tired, and I could sleep for a week after that. "I'll let you get to sleep."

"I don't want to hang up."

"I have some letters to read and a package to open before I hit the sheets myself. I have to report back at 0400."

"Okay." She's disappointed, and so am I, but this is the hand we were dealt, and we have to make the best of it. I think this phone call proved that we're good at that.

"Sweet dreams, my beautiful wife."

"I always dream of you."

"Me too, baby. I love you."

She smiles. "I love you too, my sexy husband."

I laugh at her reply. "I'll call again as soon as I can. I might not be able to call when I send pictures, but I promise you I'll send them."

"Thank you."

I shake my head. "Never thank me for doing right by you, Faith."

"But—we didn't have to do that."

"Yeah, baby, we did. We were missing each other, and it made us feel closer to each other. At least it did for me."

"Me too."

I nod. "See you soon."

"Please stay safe."

"Always."

I force myself to end the call. I have to, or else I'll stand here all night until my battery dies while I watch her sleep. I make my way back to the tent, and Erik looks up when I plop down on my cot. He sees my shirt in my hand and smirks. He grabs his phone and takes off. I have no doubt he and Hannah are about to have a similar experience. Being married and being away from my wife sucks, but I'll admit, it has its perks.

Chapter 18

Faith

I t's early October, and even though it's still warm in the Mojave Desert, I have the windows open in my classroom and am enjoying the warm breeze blowing in. I'm changing my classroom decorations over from the ones that symbolized school to Halloween. I *love* all things Halloween and am really excited about the opportunity to dress up. As a kindergarten teacher, I think it's important to join in classroom fun, which is why I've already ordered my witch costume online. It should be here in another week.

I'm about to wrap it up for a Friday afternoon when there's a knock on my door. I look up and find the principal, Mrs. Ramirez, standing in my doorway with a friendly grin. "This place looks great," she says, stepping inside and taking in the decorations.

"Thanks," I tell her. "Halloween is my favorite, so I tend to go a little overboard," I add with an awkward chuckle.

"Your kids are going to love it," she assures me.

"I hope so."

"Listen, I'm glad I caught you. I wanted to check in and see how it's going. We're about six weeks into the school year, so I thought I'd make sure everything was going the way you'd hoped."

The smile I give her is genuine and easy. "I love it, seriously. Everyone has been so helpful and supportive. I'm truly enjoying my time here."

She nods, seeming relieved. "Good, I'm glad, because the parents have been very happy with you. I know it's still early, but I'm hearing nothing but positive comments, Faith."

A blush creeps up my neck. "Thank you."

"You know my door is always open if you need anything or have concerns," she says, turning toward the door.

That's when an idea hits me.

"Actually, if you have a minute, I'd love to run an idea by you."

"Of course," she replies.

"If you'd rather it wait until Monday—"

"What's your idea, Faith?" she interrupts, smiling.

"Well, it's just that a lot of the kids here at the school are from military families, several of which are overseas right now," I start, twisting my fingers together nervously. "I was writing a letter last night to my husband, Chad, and well, the days he gets mail make him so happy. I was wondering if I could have my class work on a project—coloring pictures, writing notes, that kind of stuff—to send to his unit."

Mrs. Ramirez smiles widely. "I think that's a wonderful idea, Faith. In fact, maybe we can turn it into a whole school project. Each class can put together a care package for different units across the globe. We can write letters, collect snacks or personal hygiene items for them, and send them off."

My heart starts to pound. "Really? You think the teachers would do that?"

"I think they'd all love to be a part of it. Let me run it past them, but as far as your classroom goes, I say do it. I'm sure your parents will all be very supportive of the idea."

"Thank you," I tell her, swallowing over the sudden lump in my throat. "I might see what kind of books are available to turn it into a lesson."

She nods and continues to grin. "This sounds like a wonderful project and learning experience for your young students."

"I appreciate it," I tell her, suddenly very eager to go home and write to Chad. I don't want to give him too many details so he's surprised when he receives his package, but I want him to know how well it's going here.

"Have a great weekend," she replies before exiting my classroom, leaving me alone to finish for the day.

By the time the last ghost is hung, I'm more anxious than ever to go home. Usually, I dread it, on account the house is so quiet and lonely, but tonight, I'm eager to put pen to paper. Hell, maybe I'll try to call him and tell him over the phone. Of course, maybe we can do more of the *other* stuff too.

We haven't had phone sex since the first and only time a month ago, and I'm eager to do it again. Even though I'm touching myself, there's nothing like knowing he's observing through the phone and doing the exact same thing on the other end. Watching him stroke himself until he came was exactly what I dreamed about for several of the nights that followed.

It takes intimacy to a whole new level.

I grab my purse from my bottom desk drawer and flip off the lights to my classroom. While locking the door, I take a quick mental inventory of what's in the fridge at the house and opt to stop by the diner and grab something to take home. After dinner, I can throw on some comfy pajamas and shoot a text to Chad.

Maybe, just maybe, I'll be lucky enough to talk to him tonight.

> Me: Happy Friday, if it's Friday there. It's still Friday here, though near nine, so it might be Saturday. Just lying in bed, thinking of you. I have something big I want to share, but I'm torn by how much to tell you because I also want it to be a surprise. Isn't that silly? Anyway, just wanted to tell you good night. Stay safe. Miss you like crazy.

I set the phone down on the charger on the nightstand and look at the wedding photo in the frame. This is one Shayne snapped right when we were told Chad could kiss the bride. His hands cradle my cheeks as he stares into my eyes.

It's one of my favorite photos from our wedding day.

Then, something else hits me, and I reach for my phone again.

> Me: How many soldiers are in your unit? The thing I'm working on is going to need that info.

> Me: By the way, I talked to Ford and Shayne last night. They've set a wedding date for this spring, but you may already know that. It's in about seven months, so your deployment better hold up to the four to six months.

> Me: They also invited me home for Thanksgiving, but I don't know. I want to make sure Hannah isn't going to be here alone. If she's not going home, then I'll stay, and we'll do something together.

> Me: Or maybe I'll invite her back home with me. We don't have a long break, only Thursday through Sunday, but it might be fun to take her back with me. I'm sorry. I'm just talking at this point. Ignore me.

I set my phone down again, hoping he's not wondering what in the hell he got himself into by giving me his phone number. I don't think he'll be upset by the onslaught of messages, especially since he always complains about missing me.

I turn on the small television in the bedroom and find some cooking show. I don't really watch it, but the noise helps keep my brain somewhat calm. However, it's not really working this time, because all I can think about is the project I want to put together for Chad and the rest of his unit.

Hopping up out of bed, I grab a fresh sheet of paper and pen and start writing. I make a list of different personal hygiene items we could use, as well as individual snacks and candy. Then, I add other recreational items like decks of cards, books, crossword puzzles, sudoku books, and adult coloring books.

By the time I've completed my list, I'm smiling, hoping I can pull off even half of this project. The personal notes and pictures will be easy, since we will do those in class, but the other items on the list will require help from parents and the community. My hope is everyone rallies around the effort, since the base is at the edge of town and so many of the families at the school are affected by military deployment.

Monday, I'll write a letter to send home with the kids, and we'll see what happens.

Curling up against the pillow I've deemed Chad's, I fall into a fast sleep with thoughts of my husband filling my head.

When I wake on Saturday morning, I reach for my phone and squeal when I see Chad's name on the screen. I tap quickly, pulling up the messaging app and smile when I see his replies.

> **Husband:** First off, don't ever EVER worry about bothering me. Your ramblings are the best part of my day, and I want to hear about everything. If it goes through your pretty little head, I want to know.

> **Husband:** I think a quick trip home would be perfect for

Thanksgiving. The thought of you being there alone, especially on a major holiday, doesn't sit well with me. And taking Hannah would be great. I know Erik wouldn't want her there alone either.

Husband: I can't wait to hear more about your surprise. Part of me wants to ask for all the details now, but I also love the thought of being surprised. So you share as much info as you want and know I'll be looking forward to whatever it is you're cooking up. Oh, and there are twenty of us total in my unit.

Husband: I promise I'll do everything in my power to be home for Ford and Shayne's wedding. We should be home in plenty of time. Plus, it would be terrible if the best man was absent.

Husband: God, I miss you. You are the brightest sun in my life, and considering I'm stuck in the desert, under the hottest desert sun known to man, that's pretty telling. You. You are it, my wife. Thank you for being on this journey with me.

I wipe a stray tear off my cheek as I set my phone down. There's no reason to reply right now, especially because I know he won't have his phone on, since he powers it off to save the battery. Just as I turn to replace the phone on the nightstand, it rings. I startle, hoping it's Chad on the other end, but it's not his name.

"Good morning," I greet to Hannah.

"Hey, I didn't wake you, did I?"

"Nope. I was just reading messages from Chad."

"Aww, me too. Well, not from Chad, but from Erik. Sounds like they got back to base in the early morning. My messages arrived around 1:00 a.m."

"Mine too."

"Listen, the reason I was calling is because I'm off today. Wanna go have breakfast?"

My stomach chooses that moment to growl. "Definitely. The thought of blueberry waffles from the diner has me all sorts of ravenous," I reply with a chuckle.

"Me too. Meet me there in an hour?"

"Perfect. See you then," I say before we sign off.

I jump out of bed, eager to share my ideas with the one friend who will truly partake in my excitement because she's living this lifestyle too. I shower quickly, throwing on comfortable leggings and one of Chad's oversized Army T-shirts. I swipe a little mascara over my eyelashes and brush out my hair, pulling the wet strands back in a messy bun. Once my teeth are brushed and I've added a little powder to my cheeks, I head for the front door, locking up as I go.

The drive to the diner is short, and I'm parking my car in the small lot between it and the library within a few minutes. It's gorgeous out, and as I slip out of the driver's seat, I can't help but take a few moments to close my eyes, tip my face to the sun, and let the warmth seep into my skin.

Of course, like I do almost every other time of the day, I think of Chad. He's off somewhere in this world, baking under the hot desert sun. I hope he truly understands how proud I am of him, for doing what so few will step up and do.

I head for the front entrance and smile when I see Hannah already seated in a booth. "Hey," I greet, slipping into the bench across from her.

"Why are you so smiley? Did you and Chad get a little phone alone time?" she asks, clearly referring to phone sex.

"Uhh, no," I reply, feeling heat sweep up my neck and land in my cheeks. "I have something I'm working on though."

She leans forward with excited eyes. "Tell me."

Once we both order orange juice to drink and blueberry waffles, I proceed to share the details of my conversation with the school principal and the list of items I've come up with to send to the unit.

By the time I'm done talking, she reaches forward and squeezes my hand. "I'm in."

Chuckling, I ask, "In for what?"

"To help. I want to help," she replies eagerly. "This all sounds so amazing. I'm sure the other teachers will think it's great too. We should go to the base and find other units for care packages."

"Yeah?"

"Absolutely!" she proclaims. "I'm going to put out a donation box at the shop too. I know some of my clients will contribute. When is the deadline for items?"

"Uhh," I start, my brain starting to spin. "I didn't get that far. Do you think two weeks is sufficient?"

"Yes. If you give them any longer, they'll forget. But two weeks covers people who may not get paid every week and still want to donate items."

I nod as our food is delivered. "Thanks, Louise. This smells amazing," I tell the friendly server.

"I wasn't trying to eavesdrop, but I couldn't help but overhear what you're doing. If you make up a sign, we'll put a box up on the counter by the cash register. You may want to consider even a cash or change donation box so you can buy things you may want to add."

My throat is thick with emotion and my eyes mist over with unshed tears. "Really?"

"Absolutely! This is a small community, Faith. There are a lot of military families here, and everyone supports one another. This is a great way to do that."

I nod, unable to find my voice.

"We'll get you a sign as soon as possible," Hannah tells Louise as she dives into her waffles. When Louise walks away, she points her fork at me. "Eat. We have lots to do today."

"We do?" I ask, my heart pounding in my chest.

"Yep. We're going to the base to get more addresses, and then we're going shopping. If my husband is going to receive one of these kindergarten care packages, I'm helping."

Grinning, I can't help but say, "Thank you, Hannah. Not just for helping with this, but for… well, everything. Thanks for being my friend."

She winks. "Us military wives have to stick together."

Later that evening, I pull out a pen and fresh sheet of paper. I'm exhausted from the day, but I can't go to sleep without writing to my husband.

Dear Chad,

I'm not going to share all the details of my big surprise right now. As much as I want to, I think you not knowing is going to make it that much sweeter. Just know my entire heart is going into it.

I spent the day with Hannah, and I asked about Thanksgiving. She's going home to be with her parents and her brother and his family. She invited me to go with her, but I'm going back to Ohio. When I called my mom a little bit ago and shared the news, she informed me she's also invited your parents and sister to join us, so the only one missing will be you. You probably won't know what you're doing that day, but if you're able to call, everyone would love to hear from you. Or better yet, a video chat. This could be just wishful thinking, but a girl can hope, right? Anyway, if it doesn't work out, that's okay. There will be more opportunities.

My classroom looks amazing, all decorated for Halloween. I even found a few Halloween-themed books I'm going to read to my class as the holiday draws near. It may be silly, but I ordered a costume online, too, so when we have our classroom Halloween party and do the costume parade around town, I'll be dressed up as a witch alongside them. I can't wait.

It's dark outside, but I can see the stars so brightly out the window of our home. I hope you like what I did to the place. Everyone chipped in and helped with every room but our bedroom. I wouldn't let anyone help me there. I want your eyes to be the first to set sights on the private space I created for us.

Anyway, I'm just rambling again. Thank goodness you don't mind my senseless chatter. I haven't received a bundle of letters from you since earlier in the week, so I hope that means there's another bundle heading my way soon. Finding your letters in the mailbox is one of the best parts of my day.

Be safe.

Come home to me.

Sending all my love across the ocean and the desert,
Faith

I put today's letter in an envelope and seal it up tight. I stick it near my purse so I can drop it into the mail first thing Monday morning. With a little luck, it'll get there by next weekend. The mail system definitely has its ups and downs. Some weeks he receives a bundle with two or three letters in it, and the next week, a group of ten. It's wild how that all works.

I scan over my list of items I'm going to ask to be donated to the care packages for our troops. With a little luck, we'll be able to send a bunch of items their way. Not to mention, I'll have my class start working on their contributions to the boxes. Something tells me, a handmade item and a colored picture will go a long way with those stationed around the world, so far from home.

I have a lot to do over the next two weeks, but with Hannah helping me, I think we'll make this kindergarten project a success. And who knows, maybe we'll be able to make it an annual thing.

Of course, that would mean I receive a long-term contract, not just the one-year agreement we signed for this school year.

And I'd be okay with that. I never thought I'd find exactly what I was looking for in the Mojave Desert, but as long as Chad is here, I'm all set.

I just wish he'd hurry home.

Chapter 19

Chad

I'M OVER THE SUN. I'M OVER THE SAND, AND I'M OVER THIS FUCKING sweltering heat.

The only good coming out of this is the relationships I'm building with my unit. While patrolling a local town yesterday, I spotted two little boys out kicking an old soccer ball. I took one look at Erik, and we were both moving. We started kicking that old ball around in the dirt and sand back to the kids, reveling in the sound of their laughter. While taking a few minutes to play with the kids, I realized I wasn't worried about enemies in the area.

I knew my team had my back.

It wasn't easy forming those relationships with teammates who weren't happy with my arrival at base, but as time went on, our trust grew. I'd give my life for any one of these guys—and girls—and I know they'd do the same. That same day, other members of my unit engaged with locals, giving kids pieces of candy and always showing respect to the women and men who looked at us as outsiders, despite the fact we were there to help.

But at the end of the day, I miss my wife. I'm ready to be home with her wrapped in my arms. It's been two weeks since we've received mail. I didn't realize how much those weekly stacks of letters meant to me until I didn't receive them. Hopefully, they will get mail to us soon. I crave her words. I crave the feeling of knowing what she's up to. A few text messages here and there have gotten through, but service has been spotty at best. That might have something to do with my somber mood today. I need my Faith fix.

"Fuck, it's hot," Erik says, as we trek our way back to camp. It's been a long-ass day, and I think he's feeling the loss of mail and contact from his wife just as much as I am mine.

"Yeah," I agree. There's no point in complaining. This is what we signed up for. We knew the kinds of conditions we could potentially be working in. Regardless, it still sucks, and we're over it.

"I miss my wife," he grumbles.

"I hear ya, man. This no mail shit sucks, and cell service has been shit. The comms tent is always packed, but if I can't get her on my cell tonight, I might have to resort to that." I hate not being able to hear her voice. It's been too damn long. The comms tent offers us no privacy. There are some guys who can't get reception at all on their cell phones, even in my spot that I finally shared with them.

"Agreed. I've been thinking a lot about getting out," Erik confesses. "We want a family, and fuck me, Chad. It's hard enough being away from my wife. I can't imagine being away from my kids too. I don't want to leave her there to raise them on her own, you know?"

"I'd be lying if I said the thought hadn't crossed my mind," I confess. "Being married changes your outlook. At least it has mine." I'm proud to serve my country, but with each passing day that I'm away from her, I'm starting to think once my term is up, I'm getting out. I want a family, too, and just like Erik, I don't want my wife left behind to pick up the pieces.

I know many do, and my Faith, she would do just fine on her own. However, I don't want that. If I'm being honest, I just can't stand to be away from her. This distance is slowly killing me and the love I have for my job. I dreamed about being a soldier and serving my country. Now, all I dream about is being hers.

Just thinking about Faith pregnant with our baby sends a thrill through me. I can picture her round belly in my mind so easily. She's going to be sexy as fuck carrying my babies. Yes, babies, and yes, they're going to be mine. There is no other outcome that I'll accept where my wife is concerned. She'll find out soon enough that this marriage wasn't just for convenience. It was because my heart belongs to her, and I don't want it back.

Ever.

There are twenty of us in our team for this deployment, and it's wearing on all of us. We've trained, and we were as ready as we could be, but this heat, it's unbearable, and the sand. I have sand in places that sand should never, ever be. It's uncomfortable, and let's not talk about my feet. We walk mile after mile each day, and my feet constantly ache.

When we make it back to camp, all I want to do is strip down, take a shower, and try to call Faith. Instead, we'll have to debrief about the day's events; we have to check our gear, then we get to shower and eat, and the rest of the night is ours. We swap days and nights so much, I'm not sure which way is up. When we get home, I'm hoping I can convince Faith to take a few days off work and stay in bed with me while I catch up on sleep. Okay, maybe we won't only be sleeping. Maybe if I'm lucky, we can start working on those babies. Or at least get in some good practice. Surely, she gets vacation time, right?

Trudging into the tent, I'm ready to grab clothes and head to the shower. However, when I make it to my bed, it's covered. There are multiple boxes and a huge stack of letters. Relief swamps me. I know that most of those items are from my wife, and I crave her words. Suddenly, my exhausting shitty day just got a hell of a lot better.

"Looks like the mail finally came," one of the guys says. I don't register who as I take in the abundance of packages on my bed.

"Damn, Anthony, does your wife have a sister?" one of them asks. He peers down at the packages and letters littering my cot. Some of the guys have little or no family, and I do feel bad that I have such a great support system waiting for me at home.

I move forward, ignoring everyone and sifting through the madness. There are seven boxes in total. One of them has in big bold letters that I'm supposed to open it first. I move the stack of letters to the side and tear into the box. The first thing I see is a white envelope that says, *Read me*, so that's exactly what I do. I find the corner of the bed that's not covered, take a seat, and pull out the letter.

My dearest husband,

Surprise! I hope all the packages have reached you. There should be seven. Remember when I told you I was working on something? Well, it's turned out to be bigger than I ever could have imagined.

It all started when I went to the principal and asked if I could have my students draw pictures to send to you and your team. I thought it would be a fun project for the kids, and something that might brighten your day and the others. She said yes, but she went even further and pitched the idea to every grade level in the building.

When I told Hannah, she was on board to help. She and I spoke to someone on base who was able to give us enough addresses of deployed units that each grade level could send their own.

You get my kindergarten class, and let me tell you, they loved every minute of drawing pictures and helping pack the boxes. Hannah helped, and the outpouring of support from the community brought me to tears. Hannah took donations from her business, and other local businesses, like the diner and the pizza place, took donations as well. We split them between each grade level, and with the parents' support, I'm happy to say that each classroom was able to gather six boxes of supplies, snacks, and other fun items to send to their deployed troops.

The box you just opened, that one is just for you. Some personal supplies, some snacks, and a few other things that I thought you might like. Oh, and a couple of pictures drawn from a few of my students just for you. The other boxes are for your unit. I hope everyone enjoys the goodies. I hope that this gives all of you a little piece of home.

Speaking of home, I miss you.

All my love.
Your wife

I'm not gonna lie. I'm a little choked up at her generosity. She not only thought of me, but of every person in my unit, and the entire school pitched in. The community. I knew my wife was incredible, and this just shows the beauty that she holds inside.

And she's all mine.

"What's with all the boxes?" Timothy, one of the guys, asks.

"Care packages from my wife. Have at it. You all are welcome to anything you want. Her students drew some pictures as well. Some for each of us."

Faith didn't say that specifically, but I know my wife well enough to know she would want everyone to have one.

"Damn, you married one of the good ones, Anthony," Michaels says, as he and a few others grab a box to open them. They unpack each of them with care, placing all the items in a pile on two of the cots.

Once it's all unpacked, they take turns grabbing the things they need. The entire time, I sit on the edge of my bed. Tired, sweaty, hungry, covered in sand, my feet throbbing from the hours of walking in the desert, and a smile on my face. I'm grounded with love for the woman who holds my last name.

Suddenly, the only thing that matters is hearing her voice. Grabbing my phone, I rush out to my spot so that I can call her. It's late there, but I need to see if I can reach her. I run up the hill, and I'm panting when I dial her number. All the ailments I was just whining about in my head are long since forgotten. All I can think about is hearing her sweet voice.

"Chad?"

I sigh. "Hey, baby."

"Is everything okay?"

"It is now."

"It's good to hear your voice."

"Yeah," I agree. "I got the boxes today. I opened mine. The guys opened the others. I haven't looked through mine or read your letters, but I'm going to. I needed to call you. I needed to hear your voice and thank you. I wish you could have seen the smiles on their faces. You did that, baby. You wanted to bring us a piece of home, and you did that and so much more. Some of them, they don't get letters or packages from home. Thank you. This is an incredible surprise."

She clears her throat. "I wanted to. I'm so glad everyone liked them."

"They loved them, baby. Hell, they're asking me if my wife has a sister."

"Just a brother, and he's taken." Her laugh flows through the line.

"You're mine. Just remember that."

"Of course I am. We have the paperwork to prove it," she teases.

"You're damn right we do. We should frame it. Hang it on the wall."

"Maybe by our wedding photo."

"Did you hang one of us up in the house?" I don't know why the thought of that makes my heart race.

"Umm sure, we'll go with one." She chuckles.

"Baby, I don't care if it's a shrine to the day you became mine. I'm good with it."

"You might change your mind when you see it."

"Nah, not ever." I want her to make the house our home. I want her invested. I want the idea of her leaving to be devastating. She belongs there with me. "Hey, I was thinking. We should set up a time where I can call you while you're in class. I can wrangle a few people together in the comms tent and we can call in and thank your students for the pictures and all of the goodies."

"Really? You'd do that?"

"That's the least that we can do. I'll look at the schedule of when I'll be available while you're teaching and text it to you. It'll be fun. Besides, I'll get to see Mrs. Anthony in action with her students."

"Chad, they'll love that. They've asked so many questions about who the letters were going to. To be able to see some of you, you're going to make their day. Mine too."

"I'll take care of it. I'll text you as soon as I know something. Hopefully, service doesn't flake out on us again."

"Whenever. It doesn't have to be right away. Thank you. I'm so excited."

I can feel my face stretch with my smile. "Anything for my wife and her students."

"How was your day?"

I go on to tell her, trying not to complain too much, but still describing the heat, the sand, and the long-ass days on our feet. "I still need to shower and grab some dinner."

"Oh, I'll let you go."

"I needed to talk to you before I did anything else. I was missing you. Two weeks with no letters or calls… that's more than I ever want to do again."

"It was rough for me, too, but you'll be home soon."

"Do you get vacation time?" I ask her.

"I do. I only get four days since this is my first year, but yeah. Why?"

"I have this vision of coming home and us staying in bed for as long as possible."

Her breath hitches. Surely, she understands how much I want her in my arms, right?

"You'd want that?"

"More than anything." It's hard to convince her when I'm not there to touch her. To prove with my actions as well as my words that she's it for me.

"I'll see what I can do. You just worry about coming home safe."

"I will. I should go." I really don't want to end the call, but we only have so much time to eat before everything is cleaned up, and I really do need a shower.

"Chad?"

"Yeah?"

"Love you."

My heart expands in my chest. "I love you too, baby." I end the call because I know I'll want to spend the rest of my night talking to her, and I can't do that. Shoving my phone into my pocket, I head to the mess tent to grab some food before showering. Then I have a box and a huge stack of letters to keep me company the rest of the night. Basically, I get to spend the evening with my wife. It might just be her words, but it's the best I've got right now.

When I make it back to the tent, almost everyone has showered, and they're all eating something that came in the care packages.

"Hey," I say, gaining everyone's attention. "I was hoping we could find a time for a few of you to join me on a call. I want to call in to my wife's classroom, her kindergarten class, and thank the students for the drawings and the goodies. Any takers?"

I'm shocked when everyone in the room calls out that they're in. "All of you?"

"This is huge," Mike speaks up.

"Erik's wife helped," I tell them. Not wanting Hannah to not also get the recognition she deserves.

"Sister?" Tim asks hopefully.

"Nope."

"Damn. You assholes hit the jackpot," Stephens says, munching on a Cheeto.

"What about a brother?" Jamie speaks up.

"Faith has a brother, but he's engaged to my cousin."

"The good ones are always taken," Jamie mumbles.

"Hey," Stephens says, as if he's offended.

Jamie rolls her eyes. "I rest my case." The room erupts in laughter.

My wife and her big heart lifted the spirits of this entire unit tonight. It's been almost three months of living life beneath the desert sun and getting a little taste of home was exactly what we all needed to be revived. Our job here has been going well. I'm hopeful that we're out in a few weeks.

That would put us home before Christmas. I would give just about anything to be able to be with my wife to celebrate our first Christmas together. Regardless, I need to figure out a plan. If I can't be there, I still need to make sure she has presents under the tree.

"Hey, Erik. When you talk to Hannah, can you ask her if she's willing to help me with gifts for Faith? If we're not home by Christmas, I need for her to have something from me. I'm sure Faith would be happy to do the same for you."

"She'll be all over that. My in-laws are coming into town. I've already got my mother-in-law working on it for me. Just in case."

"Smart man. I'm learning," I tell him with a laugh.

"Nah, you've got this." He grabs his notebook to write a letter, and I know I need to do the same. However, I have a box to sift through and a big stack of letters to read. It's time to immerse myself in my wife's world until I fall asleep.

Chapter 20

Faith

"**A**RE WE READY?" I ASK MY CLASS, FEELING NERVOUS FOR THIS afternoon.

It took a little coordination to schedule today's conference call between my kindergarten class and Chad and a few members of his unit. Their CO arranged for them to use the comms tent for up to thirty minutes, but in order to make it all work during the school day, they're missing part of their breakfast time to do this. Chad wasn't worried, stating speaking with my class was more important than enjoying a full mealtime, but I still feel guilty.

"Ready!" they all holler, eagerly bouncing around as kindergarteners tend to do.

I take in the group of nineteen students. They're standing together on the reading rug, and it takes everything I have to keep them somewhat organized and in line. As soon as we start the video chat, we're going to do a quick group thing and then have a seat on the rug. We've been talking about this all week, so hopefully they remember what we've talked about and remain polite and respectful throughout the entire call.

My laptop is on my desk, with the camera facing the room, but I'm using the projector screen for the actual call. This way, all the kids can see what's going on when it connects.

With my heart pounding like a snare drum in my chest, my laptop starts to chime, indicating I have a call. The kids all respond excitedly, but before I connect, I turn around and place my index finger to my lips. "Shhhhh," I say softly. "Remember, we have to be quiet when the call connects. You'll each have an opportunity to speak in just a few minutes."

My class nods… and wiggles.

Man, I love teaching kindergarten.

I press the button and wait two very long seconds for my husband's face to fill the screen. As soon as I see him, tears fill my eyes, and a huge smile breaks out across my lips. "Hi," I croak, my throat suddenly incredibly dry.

"Hey, baby," he murmurs softly, reaching out and touching the screen. In that moment, it's as if he's touching me, running his calloused finger across my cheek.

Giggles erupt behind me, and I can't help but blush. For a brief second, it felt like we were the only two in the world, despite being so far apart.

I step back, looking up at the projection screen over my desk and make sure it's connected. The front classroom lights are off so the kids can see better, and since everything looks to be set, I move to the back of the group and stand behind my kids.

As I look at the screen, I realize Chad has several people behind him. Not just a couple like he indicated before. There are more than a dozen all standing there, all smiling at the camera. "Oh my goodness, I thought there was just going to be a few of you," I reply awkwardly.

Chad grins. "Everyone wanted to be a part of this."

"Wow, okay," I reply, clearing my throat. Suddenly, the plan I had come up with just vacates my head, and all I can do is stand here and stare at the man I love.

"Can we do the 'legiance now?" Frankie asks.

"Yes, let's start," I reply, finally finding the words. To my class, I ask, "Are you ready?"

I get a mixture of replies, as well as a lot of movers and shakers as they all place their hands over their hearts. Frankie was chosen as leader for the day because his dad is serving in the military, stationed in Japan for a brief time. He's expected to be home within the next month or two, and I made sure his unit was included in the list of care packages sent out by the school.

"You may begin, Frankie," I tell him, placing my hand over my heart.

"I pledge allegiance to the flag..."

As the kindergarteners start the Pledge of Allegiance, I watch as Chad and his unit stand at attention, place their hands over their hearts, and recite the pledge along with us. Once again, tears fill my eyes as I watch these little five- and six-year-olds interact with members of the military.

This is a moment I will never forget.

When we've completed the pledge, I say, "All right, class. Have a seat."

They all drop down, getting comfortable.

"The guys and I just wanted to tell you all how grateful we are for the care packages you sent us. I wish I could show you now, but we have your drawings all hanging around the bunk. It brightens up the tent and gives all of us a piece of home," Chad says.

"We had a lot of fun with this project, didn't we, kids?"

They all reply, "Yes!" or some version of it.

"The kids have a few questions for you guys. Is it okay if they ask?"

"Of course," Chad and a few others all reply.

"Well, the main question they have is what do you do during the day?" I ask.

"We all do a variety of jobs, but one of the main ones is research," Chad starts. "We also do a little work for another unit and help keep the area we're in secure. I can't give you too many more details, but I can tell you it's very hot where we're at and there's lots of sand, kinda like the Mojave Desert back home where you guys are."

We spend the next twenty minutes talking. Many kids ask questions, and the service men and women do their best to answer them. Some are silly, like "Do you have cats there? We have cats running around that get in the trash and make Daddy mad." Or slightly inappropriate questions, like "Do you shoot bad guys?"

Too soon, it's time to sign off so Chad and his unit can go eat breakfast. Sadness washes over me at the thought of disconnecting. Now that I have him on screen, I want to keep him there.

"Okay, class, can you tell everyone thank you for serving our country?" I ask, emotions already welling up in my eyes and throat.

"Thank you!" they holler collectively, and many start waving.

Chad and the rest of the unit smile and reply, "You're welcome."

I go to the laptop and disconnect the big screen, so it's just him and me now on the laptop. "Thank you so much for doing this," I tell him, my throat tight once more.

"Anything for you, wife," he replies with a gentle smile.

"Please tell the rest of the unit how much I appreciate them doing this. Today was something these kids will never forget."

"And what the kids did for us is something none of us will forget either," he says, once again touching the screen. Every time he does this, it's as if he's reaching right through the device and caressing my face. "I miss you so much," he whispers.

"Miss you too," I murmur softly.

"I wish I could stay and chat longer, but I need to get to the mess tent. A line is going to form soon to get in here and call home, especially after having the opportunity to chat with your class. It's such a great feeling to do this type of stuff, but it's also a reminder of what we left behind."

His words are like an arrow to my heart. "I'm sorry, I didn't even think about that aspect."

"Don't. Don't apologize. I'm the one who suggested this, remember? And when I asked for a couple volunteers, every single person in the unit stepped forward. We understand the sacrifices we make, and we deal. Not one of the service members who were in this tent just a few minutes ago feel anything other than joy after speaking with your class, babe. I promise. But as the nights start to close in on us, we all desperately want to hang on to that little slice of home as long as possible."

I nod, understanding what he's trying to say. Unfortunately, the kids behind me start to get a little rowdy, and I know our time is over. "Thank you for doing this."

"I love you, baby," he whispers.

"I love you too."

It's funny how easy those words are to say now, and I really hope he understands what they mean. Yes, I love him as a friend—my best friend, honestly—but it's so much more than that now.

He's my everything.

"Talk to you soon," he adds, before reaching for the button to disconnect the call.

"Bye," I whisper right before the screen goes blank.

As much as I want to sit here and maybe have a good cry over missing him so much, I can't. There are nineteen students ready for story time and their afternoon snack, so that's where I shift my focus. To helping grow little minds, all while mine is thousands of miles away, in the desert sand.

"What do you think of this one?"

I look up over my champagne glass and smile. Shayne is on her third wedding dress of the afternoon, and I couldn't be having more fun.

"Oh my God, you are breathtaking," I tell her, watching as she twirls in front of the wall of mirrors.

"You think?"

"The important question is what do you think?"

She grins from ear to ear. "This is the one."

"Shayne!"

I turn toward the voice and laugh when I see my mom and mother-in-law walk around the corner. They're both standing there in complete awe, staring at the beautiful bride-to-be in what I assume will be the dress she chooses.

"You are absolutely beautiful. My son isn't going to know what hit him," my mom states, making us all laugh.

"I agree. You're going to be the most stunning bride, Shayne," her aunt, Chad's mom, adds.

She studies herself in the mirror for several long seconds before nodding. "This one. I love it," she announces, earning cheers from all of us.

"Excellent," the saleslady replies. "What do you see for a veil? Waist, fingertip, floor, or chapel length?"

Shayne's eyes bug out a little bit, and I can sense there's a hint of panic happening. Quickly, I stand up and approach. "Why don't we try one of each? Then the bride can determine which length she likes with the dress."

The saleslady nods. "Excellent idea. I'll be right back," she replies, scurrying off to retrieve the veils.

"Joan and I were just admiring the mother-of-the-bride and -groom dresses. We may try a few on today," Beth states.

"Please do," Shayne replies. "That's why I wanted to get as much of this stuff done as I could this weekend, since Faith is here."

Joan looks a little unsure, twisting her hands together. Shayne steps forward, taking her aunt's hands in her own and giving them a squeeze. "Uncle Henry is giving me away because he's the closest man I have to a father. And you, Aunt Joan, are the closest thing I have to a mother. I want you both to sit in the front row, and yes, that means you get to wear a mother-of-the-bride dress, because there's no one I look at as a mother more than you."

Joan wipes away a stray tear and pulls her niece into a hug. "I love you, sweet girl."

"And I love you. Now, go. Pick out a beautiful dress that'll knock Uncle Henry on his ass."

They walk away to return to the dresses, chatting a mile a minute about their options for styles and color.

"I'm so glad you came home for Thanksgiving," Shayne states, standing in front of me.

"Me too," I tell her, taking her hand in mine.

"Chad's still gonna try to call later, right?"

I nod. "That's the plan," I reply. "I know everyone is looking forward to talking to him."

It's the Saturday after Thanksgiving, and even though we would have liked to have connected with him this past Thursday, it didn't work out with his schedule. But I received a text message early this morning, letting me know he has time this evening for a chat. He's using the comms tent again, so he knows he has a good connection and has enough time for a quick visit with the family.

"You must be looking forward to January."

My heart skips a beat. "I am," I reply instantly. Chad informed me last week they're looking to head home in early to mid-January. The exact date still isn't set, but the fact they'll be home closer to the five-month mark instead of the six makes me insanely happy.

And nervous.

"Have you told him?"

Her question catches me off guard. "Told him what?"

"That you love him, silly."

I open my mouth but close it just as quickly. Shayne is the only person I've told that our rushed wedding wasn't entirely for love. Yes, there's love there, but not the kind you plan a quickie wedding for. Our union was based on Chad's deployment to give him peace of mind and to help me settle into my first real job as a kindergarten teacher. Not exactly heartfelt reasons to tie the knot.

"I, uh…"

"That's a no."

"I've told him I love him, but I'm sure he just thinks it's because we're friends. Same with him saying it."

"He doesn't," she assures me confidently. "He tells you because he means it."

"I don't know…"

"I do. That man is head over heels in love with you, Faith. Always has been, even if you two decided to stick with friendship because of his military career."

"It's so complicated, Shayne," I whisper, dropping down into the chair behind me.

"Love always is, Faith, but no matter what journey it takes you on, the end result is always worth it. Some rides are short and reckless. Those are lessons we learn, while other loves stick their landing and stay. Like Ford. He was one determined SOB," she says with a chuckle. "And I'm so glad he fought for us, because I've never been happier than I am to walk through this life with your brother at my side."

I reach out and take her hands. "He's the lucky one."

"And so is Chad. He knows it too. I know things happened fast for you two, but don't discount the fact it's still very real. And very right. Every love is different, Faith. Just because it didn't happen like it did for someone else doesn't make it any less true."

My throat bobs as I try to swallow over the lump. All I can do is nod.

"I think you should tell him when he gets home. Tell him you *love him* love him and want to make a million babies."

And just like that, Shayne breaks the tension with a single comment.

"I'm not sure about a million. I'm not giving birth to a litter in a box under the stairs."

She smiles. "Wouldn't that be something?"

"No, that sounds terrible," I reply, laughing. "I need a hospital room with drugs. All the drugs, Shayne."

She giggles even more. "Me too."

"All right, I have several different lengths for you to try, Shayne," the saleswoman says, rejoining us in the back room.

I watch as they go through the process of trying each length with her dress. Since the back is open and there isn't a train to her dress, Shayne ultimately settles for a cathedral length, which extends out several feet onto the floor. It's also thinner and doesn't cover the detail of the dress as much as the thicker, waist-length veil did.

"That's the one," I tell her confidently. "You look absolutely stunning."

"Thanks," she says, giving herself one last look in the mirror. "March is going to be here before we know it."

"It is, but we'll be ready. I might be living a plane ride away, but I'm just a phone call away. I'll help anyway I can," I reassure her.

She nods and heads for the dressing room to change out of her dress. "Thanks, Faith, for everything."

"You're not just my brother's future wife. You're my sister too."

Tears fill her eyes as she gives me a grateful smile. "Give me five minutes to change, and then we're going to pick you out the perfect maid of honor dress."

Images of tacky, terrible dresses filter through my mind, and I'm so grateful Shayne isn't the type to want anything other than something simple, classic, and beautiful.

With excited grins on our faces, we set out to find the perfect maid of honor dress.

One that will hopefully bring Chad Anthony to his knees.

Chapter 21

Chad

MY KNEES ARE BOUNCING.

My heart is racing.

My hands are itching.

Three days ago, our CO informed us that we were going home. Just a week before, he'd told us we'd be rolling out after the first of the year. I called my wife to tell her as soon as I found out. That changed, and now here we are. It's the week before Christmas, and I'm going home to my wife.

She has no idea.

I don't think I've ever been this excited about seeing someone in my entire life. The bounce of my knees is me wanting to run to her. My racing heart, that's the love I have for the woman who took my name just over four months ago. And my itching hands? It's because I can't wait to hold her.

Not long now.

The bus slows, and we turn into the base. I don't have to look at a single face on this bus to know we're all feeling the same way. We're glad to be home. What's even better is that my wife doesn't know that I'm coming.

I'd already told her it would be after the first of the year. When we were told three days ago that had changed, there was a lot of work to do. So, I focused on that because I wanted to surprise her.

The bus stops, and we quickly unload. I have to report tomorrow for a few hours, but then we're off until after the new year. I've never been more thrilled to know my wife is a teacher, and she too will be home. No need for her to take her vacation days.

"It's good to be home," I tell Erik as I follow him off the bus. The last part of the ride, we were both quiet. Hell, the entire bus was quiet. We're all exhausted and ready for home.

"Yeah," he agrees. We toss our bags over our shoulders and begin the short walk to our houses. Faith had already told me that Erik and Hannah don't live far from us. Luckily, the base is well lit for a night walk, and to be honest, I need this time to calm the hell down. I'm nervous and excited, and I need to get those feelings under control before I knock on our front door.

Yeah, I'm gonna knock. I can't wait to see her face when she sees that it's me.

As we approach the house, I know it's ours, not only from the numbers on the house, but the car in the driveway. This is it. I'm home.

"I'll see you in the morning."

Erik chuckles as I wave him off. I've spent the last several months with him. It's time for my wife to have all my attention. "See ya!" he calls over his shoulder.

Dropping my bag onto the front porch, I wipe my sweaty palms on my thighs before lifting my hand and knocking on the door. I hear footsteps inside, and then I see the curtain move to the side. A squeal of excitement greets me as the door is tugged open, and my wife is jumping into my arms.

I catch her easily as she wraps her arms and legs around me and buries her face in my neck. Her body shakes and I can feel her tears against my skin. I hold her close, so tight. In fact, I'm sure I'm probably squeezing the air from her lungs, but Faith doesn't seem to mind. I squeeze my eyes closed to ward off my own onslaught of emotions. I focus on the feel of her in my arms.

Finally.

"You're here." She lifts her head and smiles through her tears. "How are you here?" Her eyes roam over my face as if she has to catalog my every feature.

Don't worry, baby. We have a lifetime for that.

"Let's get you inside." I step through the door that's still open, kicking it closed. I look around her just so I can take us to the couch before sitting with her still wrapped around me.

"Let me look at you." I cradle her cheeks in the palms of my hands and stare into her eyes. "I've missed you." My voice cracks. The relief of having her in my arms again is palpable. She's the missing piece of me.

"I missed you too. I didn't know you were coming." Surprise colors her voice, and her smile tells me it's a good one.

"We found out three days ago. It's been a whirlwind. We were all doing whatever we needed to do to get out of there and come home. I could have made the time to call, but I wanted to surprise you," I confess.

"Best Christmas present ever." She grins.

Not able to stand it a second longer, I lean in and press my lips to hers. My tongue glides along her lips, taking my fill. She opens for me, and I don't hesitate to taste her fully, allowing our tongues to dance. I lose track of time as we continue to kiss. My hands roam over every single part of her that I can reach. When she rocks her hips, we both moan in pleasure. I need to slow this down. I want to see the home she's made for us.

"Show me what you've done to the place." I don't want to stop. However, I know we need to talk. I need her to know that when I tell her that I love her, it's not only because she's my best friend. I can't let us get sidetracked before we have that conversation. I don't want to go to bed another night without this incredible woman knowing what she means to me.

"Okay. Just know that I can change anything you don't like."

"Baby, I'm sure it's fine. Let me grab my bag from the porch and then I want the tour." I kiss her again, because I can. Because she's here in my arms where she belongs. I have a few years left, and in that time, I'm probably going to have to leave her again. I hope like hell by some miracle I don't.

I do know that once my time is up, I'm done. That's something else I need to talk to her about. However, first, I need to see the home she created for us.

She stands and takes my hand, walking with me to the door to grab my things. I leave them inside on the floor and give my wife my full attention.

"This is the living room." She smiles softly.

I let my eyes roam around the room and stop when they land on an enlarged wedding photo of us. "That"—I point to the photo—"is my favorite part."

She squeezes my hand, resting her head on my shoulder from her spot next to me. "Yeah, that's my favorite too."

We continue on to each room. I see her touch in every single one of them. What I also see is me. She has my PlayStation set up in the living room. There are pictures of us everywhere. My running shoes are next to the front door beside hers, and she has a framed photo of her on my side of the bed on the nightstand. In the bathroom, there are his and hers sinks, and all my products are organized neatly. She was just waiting for me to come home.

Emotion wells in my throat. I force myself to swallow over the lump.

It feels so fucking good to be home.

"Well?" Faith asks. She's peering up at me as she bites down on her bottom lip. She's worried I won't like what she's done with the place. What she doesn't understand is that as long as she's living here, I couldn't care less what she does with it. If she's in that bed next to me every single night, she can paint our room hot pink with purple polka dots for all I care.

"You did great, baby." I bend to place my lips on hers.

Now that I've had the tour, we need to have that talk. Our bed is calling my name, and I'm not going to sleep until I know that she's going with me every night for the rest of our lives.

"We need to talk," I tell her. Instantly, her body stiffens.

"Right." She nods. "It's fine, really. I have the guest room all set up as you saw, so I can move in there until I find a place." She tries to pull away, but my hold on her is firm.

It takes me a few moments to register what she just said. "Wait. What?" I ask her. She tries to step away again, but I'm faster, keeping a tight grip on her hand, and pulling her into my chest. I wrap my other arm around her waist, keeping her close. "Faith?"

"It doesn't have to be complicated."

She won't look at me.

"What are you talking about?"

"You're home now. This—" she waves her hand between us in the little space that's left "—was temporary. I should move to my own room." Her eyes are locked on my chest.

"Fuck that."

She stills, and her breath hitches. I place my hand beneath her chin so that her eyes meet mine.

"Is that what you want? Do you want to move out of our room?"

"It's your room, Chad. I'm a guest here."

"The hell you are." I scoop her up in my arms and carry her to the bed. I place her down gently and climb above her. My hands rest beside her head, and I'm nestled between her thighs where I belong. "You are not a guest here. This is your home. *Our* home."

She nods, and tears form in her eyes. "But it's not real."

"Does this feel real?" I rock my hips into her pussy. "Does this feel real?" I bend my head and kiss her soft lips. Keeping one hand braced on the bed, the other takes her hand and places it over my heart. "Does this feel real?"

"Chad—"

I rock my hips again, and she arches her back. "Real," I tell her. Lowering my head, I capture her lips with mine, this time kissing her with everything I've got. By the time I pull away, we're both panting. "So fucking real," I murmur, kissing her again. "And this." I tap my hand over hers that's still resting over my heart. "It beats for you. Only you."

She blinks a few times, trying to clear her eyes from the tears. "I don't understand."

She does understand. I can see the hope in her eyes. They're not just filled with hope; there is love shining back at me. I fucked up. I should have told her before I left, but that's all right. I'm going to fix it.

Climbing off the bed, I offer her my hand.

"What are you doing?"

"Humor me, baby."

She does as I ask, placing not only her hand, but her trust in me as she allows me to help her stand from the bed as well. I hold her hands in mine and stare into her eyes.

"You're beautiful." Her eyes soften. Wrapping my arms around her, I hug her tight. My heart feels as though I just ran a mile as fast as I could go. Stepping back, I drop to my knees. Not just one, both.

"What are you doing?"

"I love you."

"I love you too."

"You're my best friend. You're the most important person in my life. You're my wife."

"Chad—"

"My love for you is infinite. It will never waver, and it can only grow stronger. This is our home, Faith, but what you don't realize is that *you* are my home. I don't care where we live as long as you're next to me. I want all your days and all your nights." Leaning in, I place a kiss on her belly. "I want to make a family with you. I want it all. I want my wife."

A small sob falls from her lips, but I keep going. I need her to understand.

"Mrs. Faith Anthony, will you do me the incredible honor of marrying me—again? We'll do it right, baby. We'll have the big wedding and the beautiful gown, all the guests, the wedding party, the reception, the honeymoon—all of it. I want to give you what I couldn't before. I want to give you the world. You already have all of me."

She tugs on my hands, and I stand. With my thumbs, I wipe the tears from her cheeks, but they continue to fall. "I wouldn't change any of it. Not a minute. It's our story, husband."

I smile at that, and in turn, so does she.

"I don't need another wedding. I don't need a fancy dress or a big reception. I don't need the honeymoon. I just need you. You are all I've ever wanted. You are my world. You have all of me. My love for you is infinite."

"You're mine, Mrs. Anthony. Where you go, I go. I have a few years left in my contract, but after that, I want out. I know there's a pretty good chance during that time, I'll have to leave you again. However, after that, never again. It's you and me, baby."

Her smile lights up her face. "You are my greatest gift."

"Yeah? You feeling up to another one?"

"All I need is you."

"Well, you're in luck. I'm giving you me." I step back and pull my shirt over my head, tossing it to the floor. Her eyes rake over my body, and my cock has never been this hard. "I want to make love to my wife."

"What are you waiting for?" She starts stripping out of her clothes, and all I can do is stand back and watch the show. "Too many clothes, husband. Strip."

"Yes, ma'am." I strip out of the rest of my clothes quickly. Reaching down, I grip my cock, squeezing the base. "It's a good thing you're already mine. This is about to be embarrassing."

She giggles. "We have a lifetime, right?"

"Damn right." Bending, I grip the back of her thighs, and she wraps her arms and legs around me. I stand frozen for just a minute, relishing the feel of her skin against mine. Reaching between us, I rub my thumb over her clit to find her wet. "You're ready for me." I take a seat, feeling her heat hover over me.

"Please."

"Please, what, baby?"

"Take the ache away."

"Anything for my wife." Gripping my cock, I guide myself inside her. She pushes down, and we both moan at the feeling of being one after all the months we spent apart.

"Take me. Take what you need. I'm already close, just feeling your skin against mine."

"It's going to be quick, but I promise you, I'll make love to you all night long."

"Then you better fuck me first."

"Hold on, wife." My hands move to her ass as I grip them tight. She squeals when I lift her up and bring her back down on my cock. "I fucking missed you."

"This—and you," she pants.

I grin as I plant my feet and slam her back down on my cock. Her head rolls to the side, her hair falling down her back. I want to bury my fist in it, but right now, all I can do is grip her fine ass and pull her down on me over and over again.

This is heaven.

This is my future.

"Chad—Oh!" she moans. The sound comes from somewhere deep in her chest.

"Tell me what you need, baby. I'm close." Tingles race down my spine, and my balls tighten. I'm barely hanging on. I can't come before her or without her.

I. Just. Can't.

"There. Right—there. Yes. Yes. Yes!" She screams the last one, and her pussy clamps down on my cock. The pressure is the most perfect fucking feeling, and I can't hold on. I release into her as she holds onto me, and we both ride out wave after wave of pleasure.

"Welcome home, husband."

"I love coming home to you, wife."

"Forever."

"Forever, baby."

Epilogue

Faith

March

THIS WEEKEND HAS BEEN ABSOLUTELY AMAZING.

Shayne is the most beautiful bride, and I'm certain I'll never forget the way my brother looked at her when he first spotted her walking down the aisle. It was the type of scene you read about in romance novels. They were pronounced husband and wife, had a million photos taken, enjoyed a delicious meal, and are now wrapped up in each other's arms as they sway to another slow song.

And me?

I'm gently moving to the beat with my own arms wrapped around the man I love.

My husband.

There's no place else I'd rather be, except for maybe naked in bed with him, but we can get to that later.

Smiling, I keep watching my brother and sister-in-law. Part of that is because they're so stinking cute and lovey-dovey, but there's another reason. Every time I look at my husband, I want to blurt out the secret I've been keeping since right before we left to fly home for the wedding. As much as I want to tell him, I don't want to ruin anything for anyone else, so I'll keep my mouth shut until we get home.

"What's wrong?" he murmurs, his warm breath tickling my ear.

"Nothing," I insist, letting him pull me closer against his hard body.

He gently places his fingers below my chin and lifts so our eyes connect. The moment they do, a wave of guilt sweeps through me, and I almost blurt it out.

Suddenly, we stop dancing, and he takes my hand in his. He escorts me off the dance floor and out the door of the reception venue. The cool March air hits us, and a chill slides through my body. We walk to the side, away from the door, and stop. He spins around, taking his suit jacket off and hanging it over my shoulders. The warmth feels good, and I instantly give him a grateful grin.

"Thanks," I tell him, breathing in the scent of his cologne clinging to the jacket.

"Always, love." He levels me with a stern look. "Now tell me what's wrong."

I open my mouth and shake my head. "Nothing's wrong. I promise."

"But there's something. I can tell."

"How?"

He flashes me a cocky grin. "I know my wife. I can tell when something's bothering her or causing her concern. You worry your bottom lip, which you've been doing all weekend. So, what gives?" Chad pulls me into his arms and places a kiss on my forehead.

I sigh, relaxing into his embrace. "I wasn't going to tell you until we're back home Monday," I mutter, resting my cheek against his chest.

"Tell me now."

I meet his concerned gaze. There's no way he's going to let this slide.

Straightening my spine, I speak the words I've been holding on to since I peed on the stick Thursday morning. "I'm pregnant."

His face remains completely impassive for what feels like a thousand years, but in reality is probably two seconds. It's as if realization hits him when he whoops and hollers in excitement and throws his arms up in the air. He smiles widely, picks me up around the waist, and spins me around twice. In the excitement, his suit jacket falls from my shoulders.

"You're pregnant? Really?" he asks the moment he sets me down on the ground.

"Yes," I tell him, laughing.

Chad slams his lips against mine, kissing me soundly. "I can't believe it," he murmurs, reaching down and placing both hands against my still-flat stomach. "*My baby*. My baby and my wife." He's smiling so big, it might border on painful.

"I just found out Thursday. I was a few days late, and I got a little… excited."

"*My baby*," he practically sings, pulling me into his arms and kissing me once more. "We're having a baby."

"I was going to tell you, promise, but I didn't want to take anything away from Shayne and Ford's wedding weekend. I figured I'd tell you when we got home, and then we can tell everyone else in a few weeks."

The door to the reception hall opens and behind us I hear, "I told you they probably slipped outside for nooky," Ford grumbles.

I snort and shake my head. "Aren't you two supposed to be receptioning right now?" I ask.

The newlyweds stop in front of us, Ford holding his wife firmly against his chest. "Shayne was worried, so we thought we'd come make sure everything was all right."

"Worried?" I ask, giving her my attention.

"I saw the looks on your faces when you quickly walked off the dance floor. I could tell something was wrong," she says reasonably. "Spill."

"It's nothing," I say, repeating the same thing I had said to Chad.

Problem is, Chad speaks at almost the exact same time. "Faith's pregnant."

I gasp and spin around to face him. "We weren't saying anything," I whisper-yell.

He's smiling ear to ear and laughs. "I'm not sorry. I've been waiting months to say those words," he states with a cocky smile.

"You're pregnant?" Shayne asks.

I quickly turn back around and face my brother and sister-in-law. "Yes, but that doesn't matter. This is your weekend. We won't say a word to anyone," I reassure her, hoping she doesn't think I'm trying to upstage her.

"You're pregnant?" she asks again, seeming a little shocked. "Holy crap, we're going to be pregnant together?"

"Yes, but—wait, what?" I gape at her, trying to understand exactly what she's saying.

Shayne smiles. "I found out last week, but we decided not to say anything until after the wedding."

My twin steps up, pulling her into his arms again and adds, "This way we can tell everyone it was a honeymoon baby."

I chuckle and throw my arms around them. "Oh my God, I can't believe it! You're pregnant too?"

"Yep! This is going to be so amazing," she replies, hugging me tightly as Ford goes to shake Chad's hand.

"Knocked up my twin sister. I'm not sure how I feel about this," Ford teases, giving him the eye.

"Knocked up my wife, Gregory," Chad corrects. "Congrats," he adds, pulling his friend into a hug.

"Wow, I can't believe this. Both pregnant at the same time. Our babies are going to be not only cousins, but the best of friends," Shayne says, linking her arm through mine and slowly walking us back to the reception.

"Hey, you two go on in. I need one more minute with my wife," Chad says as we reach the door.

"Fine, but no nooky," Ford grumbles, taking Shayne's hand and leading her back into the reception.

"No promises!" Chad hollers, earning a middle finger right before Ford disappears through the door.

"Come here, wife," he says, pulling me into his arms once more. "Are you happy?"

I nod. "Very. I know we weren't actively trying, but I guess we weren't preventing it either."

"No, we were trying. I was very much trying to put a baby in your belly. The moment you stopped taking birth control, it became my mission."

Smiling, I shake my head and rest my cheek against his chest. I can hear the pounding of his heart and revel in the strong beat. "Well, whatever you want to call it, it worked."

He grins wolfishly. "It was that night against the kitchen table. I gave you all my best moves that night, baby."

My cheeks flush at the memories his words evoke. I'd never pictured myself getting bent over our table, but I'll definitely never forget it anytime soon. Slipping my hands up his jaw and into his hair, I press my lips against his. "I love you, husband."

"Love you, wife. More than ever."

Epilogue

Chad

5 years later

I STEP THROUGH THE FRONT DOOR AND LISTEN.

Coming home at the end of a busy shift is my favorite part of the day. Nothing beats the sounds home brings, especially the few minutes after I walk through the door.

"Daddy!" hollers our four-year-old son, Austin, the sound of his running feet hitting the hardwood floors follow in his wake.

I drop my bag and take a knee just before he comes barreling around the corner and flies into my arms. "How's my favorite little man?" I ask, kissing his forehead.

It's in that moment I realize he must have been snacking on something sticky and wet, because ten tacky fingers touch my face as he gives me a wide, toothy grin. "I dood."

"Where's your sister and mama?" I ask, picking him up and holding him to my chest as I go in search for the rest of my family.

"Bewwies!" Austin bellows, pointing to the kitchen.

I step inside the kitchen and stop in my tracks. Abigail sits in the high chair, eating freshly cut strawberries and blueberries, and my beautiful wife is standing at the sink, washing dishes. It's the most normal thing in the world, but it means more to me than I ever thought anything could.

"Dada!" Abigail proclaims, pointing at me from her chair. She's smiling, having just turned two, and makes the motion for me to pick her up.

"Finish your snack, and then I'll get you out of there, bug," I tell my daughter, kissing the crown of her dark head before setting Austin back in his booster seat. "Finish eating your berries, and then I'll help you get washed up."

"'Kay!"

I turn toward the sink and smile. Faith is watching me, leaning against the counter. My cock takes notice of her tight leggings and her fitted top, stirring to life at the sight of her. "Hello, my wife."

She steps forward and throws her arms around my neck, kissing my lips. I can taste strawberry, one of her favorite afternoon snacks these last few weeks. "Hello, my husband," she whispers, wrapping her arms around my waist.

I slide my hands down her back and around her sides until they land on the swell of her stomach. "How's my baby treating you today?"

Faith is five months pregnant with baby number three, and though she swears this is it, I'm secretly hoping I can convince her to have more. Faith is not only the best kindergarten teacher I know, but she's the best mother too.

"She's been playing bongos on my bladder," Faith grumbles, but quickly smiles.

Bending down, I put my mouth right beside her belly and say, "Listen here, Alex Morgan, I'm going to need you to stop abusing your mama's bladder." I then place a loud kiss on her belly, as I do every time

I get home from work. Or when I leave. Or just randomly, because seeing my wife's pregnant stomach is the sexiest fucking thing in the world.

And cue my cock once more...

"Maybe that's what we'll name her. Alex."

"It's fitting," I reply, gently rubbing up her back and massaging her shoulder blades.

"Oh, God," she moans, closing her eyes and swaying into me. "That feels so good."

I snort. "You're turning me on," I whisper so little ears can't hear.

She chuckles and lets me work over the knots in her shoulders. "How was work?" she asks, keeping her eyes closed.

"Not bad. A few traffic stops and a domestic call," I tell her.

"I don't like you responding to those," she mutters.

I know she worries about it, but it's the job.

After being honorably discharged from the military, I promptly enrolled in the police academy in Ohio, where we finally relocated to. Moving back near our family was the right move for us, especially with our son. Faith was desperate to be close to her mom and dad, as well as Shayne and Ford, and we're a short drive away from my family in Kentucky.

She was able to find a kindergarten position right here in Cooper, which was a dream come true for her. She's one of two teachers at that grade level, her mom being the other.

I graduated from the academy and secured a job through our local Cooper PD. I just completed my probationary period and am out patrolling solo. I enjoy my job. It gives me that sense of pride in being able to give back to my community and allows me to not only provide for my family, but I'm home with them every night. Daddy no longer has to leave for months at a time, and I never will. Not unless Faith and our kids are with me. I can't go that long without them. Never again.

We've settled into this stage of our life with ease, and every day brings new memories and new adventures. I can still remember the day

I married her, and I thought I couldn't love her more, but I was wrong. My wife, she's a part of me. She's the other half of my soul. She's given me two, soon to be three, and hopefully more beautiful children, in addition to her heart. There are no greater gifts than that.

No more long hot days beneath the desert sun. No more letters or grainy video calls. No more living for mail day. Instead, I come home to this. My wife and kids who are just as excited to see me as I am them.

My family. My heart. My world.

Bonus Material

Faith

Dear Chad,

Our families left today. The house is quiet as I sit here and process the last few days. The house is great, and I think you're going to love it. It came furnished, but you already knew that. I went shopping with our moms, Shayne, and your sister. We bought rugs, a couple of lamps, picture frames, and other odds and ends to make this place a home.

Our home.

We're married. It all seems like a dream to me. One minute, you're here, and we're saying our vows. The next, I'm saying goodbye as you head to the desert. However, the weight of my wedding band tells a different story. One that's true and everlasting.

I miss you.

Love,
Faith

Chad,

Have I told you how much I love being a kindergarten teacher? I do. So much. Today was an interesting day, to say the least. Each week, a new student is selected for show-and-tell. They are allowed to bring something with them to show the class. It can be anything they want. Last week, Stella and her mom brought their pet bunny. The kids loved it.

This week, however, was more entertaining for me, at least until I had to tell Nicholas's mom what he brought when she picked him up. I'm still laughing about it as I write this.

So, I called Nicholas up to the front of the class. He ran to his cubby and grabbed his Thor backpack. He skipped to the front of the class and beamed a smile at me. He announced to the class that he had brought his lightsaber to show them. Sounds cool, right?

It wasn't cool—not at all—not for a kindergarten class. You see, Nicholas didn't bring a lightsaber after all. No, he brought a light-up vibrating dildo. He whipped it out of his backpack and swung it around in the air over his head. The kids were fascinated when he told them it shook.

I kid you not.

Here I am, trying my hardest not to laugh and hurt his feelings while this five-year-old is swinging his mom's light-up vibrating dildo in the air to show his classmates. This is an incident they didn't prepare me for in college.

I quickly directed the class to an art activity I knew they would all love. Nicholas was bummed he had to put his lightsaber away. I told him he could show it to his mom when she picked him up. He was appeased by that, but his mother, on the other hand, was not. I'm terrible, and I know this. What else was I supposed to do? I was at a loss and needed it to go back into his backpack and away from all the kids.

Let me tell you, there is never a dull moment with these littles.

I should let you go. I have laundry to do and still need to make something for dinner. I couldn't wait to tell you about my day.

Stay safe.

Love you.

Faith

❧

Chad,

I've been staring at the shadows on the bedroom ceiling for over an hour. I can't stop thinking about our phone call yesterday. How can you be thousands of miles away in the desert yet still feel as though you're here with me? This might sound crazy, but my hands could have been yours with your deep, gruff voice coming over the line.

I've never done anything like that before, and I've never wanted to. I've never met a man I felt safe enough with whom I could trust to be that open—not until you. I'm missing you extra hard tonight. I wish you were here lying next to me.

I can't believe I'm going to admit this, but honesty in a marriage is important. I tried tonight. I tried touching myself, pulling up images of yesterday in my mind, but it's not the same. Not without you.

I might be broken. I'm not me without you. Then again, maybe I'm not broken. Maybe I'm finally whole. Either way, I know that I miss you terribly.

All my love,

Faith

Chad,

Today sucked. It started out fine. It was an ordinary day, but it quickly went downhill. Just after lunch, Chloe approached my desk, telling me she didn't feel well. Before I could even suggest we send her to see the nurse, she bent over and puked all over my shoes.

She was crying, and I felt like crying. Other students were gagging and laughing, and it was out of control. I texted the principal and the janitor to send someone to cover my class. I got Chloe to the nurse and went to the staff restroom to salvage my shoes. I cleaned them off, but then I was walking around in cold, wet shoes all day.

It was not a pleasant experience.

Anyway, it gets worse. At the end of the day, as soon as I got into my car, I turned on an audiobook I'd been listening to. I needed to disappear into another world. I also decided that I deserved an iced coffee after the day I had, so I pulled into the coffee shop drive-thru, which was surprisingly packed at that time of day. I was content to sit my turn in line and listen to my book.

This is where it gets interesting. I pull up to the order kiosk and hit pause on my phone. At the same time, I roll the window down on the car. In theory, this was a grand plan. Yeah, not so much. You see, my phone didn't pause. I know what you're thinking. What's the big deal? The big deal is that I was at a spicy scene in the book. So, through the speaker, the attendant taking my order heard more than I'm sure he bargained for when he asked to take my order. I fumbled with the knobs and turned off the radio, but that wasn't good enough. It was still playing through my phone!

I was finally able to get the book to stop. I contemplated driving off, but I really wanted that iced coffee. I ordered and pulled forward. I think my face was just as red as the teenage boy's who took my order. I paid, gave the poor kid a tip, mumbled a thank-you, and drove off. So, yeah, I can never show my face there again. Not ever.

I'm headed to the shower and then to bed. I'm glad this day is over.

Missing you.

Faith

To my sexy husband,

I had the best night. Hannah came over for dinner, and we had some wine. We just talked and chatted about anything and everything. It was so much fun. We made plans to go shopping tomorrow.

She told me that she and Erik want to have a baby. I love babies, but I'd only want to have them with you. You know, because we're married and all that.

Did I tell you we had wine? Three bottles of wine. Hannah is asleep on the couch, but I couldn't go to sleep before I wrote you a letter. I vowed to love you, and honor you, and cherish you, and write you a letter every day.

Obey, do you think that means in the bedroom? Because we both know I'd do whatever you told me to in the bedroom. Speaking of bedrooms, we need another one of those sexy time calls. We need lots of those.

Maybe we could have a baby? A cute little boy who looks just like his daddy. Do you want to have babies with me?

I'm going to put this in an envelope tonight and slip it in the stack, so I don't read it in the morning and not send it.

I'm so tired, and the words are starting to blur.

I need sleep.

I need you beside me.

I love you.

Faith

Bonus Material

Chad

My beautiful Faith,

Today was a hard day. I've been gone a week, and even though they're keeping us plenty busy, I can't stop thinking about you. You've crept into my mind so much, it's almost a distraction. The best kind of distraction, but one, nonetheless. I almost dropped a barbell while working out with my team, because my mind was reliving our wedding day—or more specifically, the wedding night. I knocked over a bottle of water onto my food tray at dinner and soaked it all, making it inedible. And then I went to shower and left my travel bag behind. Didn't notice it either until I was under the spray and reached for my shampoo. Which I didn't have.

I miss you.

Terribly.

So much so it hurts to breathe.

You're a part of my soul.

Exactly what I need to get through every day here until I see you again.

But I admit, it's hard not to long for that time. It's been a week, and I'm already miserable.

Hopefully tomorrow will be better, because each day is one closer to you.

All my love,
Chad

My beautiful wife,

I'm not a fan of pranks, Faith. At all. But it seems like the thing to do to help pass the time around this place. It was all fun and games while the team pulled their juvenile bullshit on everyone else, but then they turned their jokes on me.

I can't believe I'm about to tell you this, but you're my wife and I tell you everything, so here goes.

I was in the can, minding my own business, when I realized there was no TP. And no one else was in there. I was so relieved when I actually had enough cell reception to send an SOS to Erik. He comes running over to the bathroom but proceeds to tell me there's no TP in any of the stalls. None. What the hell?! So he has to go to the supply tent and see if he can find some.

Five minutes go by.

Then ten.

Fifteen.

And there I sit, impatiently waiting.

Finally, he comes back and says he found some. And that's when I hear the snickering. A roll of toilet paper gets passed over the door. Only problem is…it's wet. Soaking wet, Faith. So I holler for Erik or someone else to knock it off, and they proceed to pass me five more rolls of toilet paper, and yes, they're all wet.

Assholes.

I work with assholes, Faith.

Every one of them.

Let's just say, I learned a valuable lesson that night. I take my own TP to the toilet with me.

At least it wasn't itching powder in your boxers. Which reminds me, send me some itching powder. I have the perfect use for it…

I've been learning a lot about the people around me. There are twenty of us in total. Eighteen men and two women. Seven are married, while the remaining thirteen are either single or dating someone. A few have kids already, but not many. Just wait, though. You pull a man away from his wife or girlfriend for up to six months and when he returns home, babies will be made.

All right, they're hollering for me again. We're playing cards tonight, and the winner gets thirty minutes of uninterrupted use of the comms tent tomorrow to call home. Wish me luck, wife.

Talk to you soon, baby.

Love,
Chad

Best. Day. Ever.

Hello, dear wife,

I'm gonna jump right into it, because it's too exciting not to share. Stephens was sent to the comms tent after getting an urgent text from his wife. They've been married the longest of the seven of us. Five years, I think, but that's not important. He was freaking out a little, terrified something was wrong at home, so a few of us went with him, just in case he needed support. None of us had any idea what we were walking into. We silently stood back, away from the view of the camera, but close enough we could be there for Stephens if we needed.

His wife appeared on the screen, and even though we tried to give them privacy, we realized quickly her tears were of joy. She held up a pregnancy test, Faith. A positive one. She told her husband they were having a baby, and it was the best moment to witness. We've been gone a month and somehow that lucky SOB knocked up his wife before he left.

He pulled us into big hugs, not caring his wife was still there, watching. We left them alone to talk, and when we got back to the bunk tent, someone started handing out cigars. I'm guessing they came from Carter. He smokes them every now and again back behind the mess tent. Anyway, when Stephens finally returned, we all went out and smoked a cigar. I know you're probably supposed to wait until the baby is born, but we make do with what is given to us, and it felt right. Plus, it brought us all together. We sat out under the night sky for hours, bullshitting and smoking those nasty cigars. But I wouldn't trade it for anything.

Anyway, it's late. Way past normal time for shuteye. We're all gonna be dragging ass tomorrow for sure, but that's okay. Seeing the smile on Stephens's face will be worth the exhaustion tomorrow.

Miss you.

More than I could ever explain in a letter.

Just know you're always on my mind, like a tattoo on my brain.

Love,

Chad

Hello, my wife,

I'm not going to beat around the bush. Today was rough.

We were working our way through a training exercise in the middle of nowhere, five miles from our extraction site. Literally nothing but desert around us. It was the worst kind of brutal conditions I could imagine. We stopped to take a breather beside a somewhat shaded hill of sand, and while we were resting, Rodriguez got stung by a scorpion. We were all on the lookout for poisonous snakes, and this little bugger came out of nowhere. Stung him on the hand when he placed it on the ground.

We've all been well trained on basic triage for just about everything we could encounter while on this deployment, but none of us were prepared for Rod to have some sort of reaction to the sting. What should have been some swelling, tingling, and numbness quickly turned to profuse sweating, abdominal pain, and an increased heart rate. I gave him a shot for pain, but we knew he needed to get back to base immediately for medical care.

That's when we threw him over our shoulders and ran back to base.

We all took turns, running and carrying our teammate all the way back. Larsen was a distance runner in high school, so she and Erik took off ahead of us to get everything prepped for our arrival, and the moment we returned, they were able to give him the treatment he needed. The man had an allergic reaction of some sort to the sting, and thanks to our fast thinking and ability to run five miles in the sweltering heat, carrying a full-grown two-hundred-and-twenty-pound man, we got him back for aid to be rendered.

And while the event had a positive outcome, it was a reminder of how quickly things can change here. How fast a young, healthy individual can become sick and require medical help, and we're the only ones to give it.

This is a crazy job I have, and while I hate the fact it pulls me away from you for far too long, I'm still proud of what I do and why I do it.

Missing you like crazy, but I gotta go now.

After that run and helping carry my teammate, I need a shower. And bed.

Love,
Chad

Wife,

Yes.

All of it, yes.

I want babies.

Lots of babies.

The thought of you drunk and thinking about me, pleasuring yourself, has me so hard I can barely write, let alone think of anything but you. Naked. In our bed. Whenever you need my hand, it's yours. Even though I'm not physically beside you, I'm there in spirit, love. And when you need me, call. I'll guide your hands as if they were my own, watching as you come undone for no one but me.

You own me.

Always.

Love,
Husband

Thank you
Thank you for taking the time to read
Beneath the Desert Sun.

www.kayleeryan.com
www.laceyblackbooks.com

There are so many people who are involved in the publishing process. We write the words, but we rely on our editors, proofreaders, and beta readers to help us make them the best they can be.

Those mentioned above are not the only members of our team. We have photographers, models, cover designers, beta readers, formatters, bloggers, graphic designers, author friends, our PA, and so many more. We could not do this without these people.

Special Thanks: Becky Johnson, Hot Tree Editing.
Deaton Author Services and Kara Hildebrand, Jo Thompson, Julie Deaton, and Jess Hodge Proofreading
Y'all That Graphic – Book Cover Boutique
Golden Czermak – Lindee Robinson Photography
Chasidy Renee – Personal Assistant
Jo, Sandra, Jamie, Stacy, Lauren, and Erica
Bloggers, Bookstagrammers, and TikTokers
Graphics by Stacy and Ms. Betty Graphics
The entire Give Me Books Team
And our amazing Readers